A LOVE LIKE OURS

The white coat had slipped from her shoulders. She was wearing the short black and white chiffon dress with the long transparent sleeves and charming ruffles around the wrists, that he had admired at dinner. He stared at her, as though fascinated. With her disordered hair and flushed cheeks she looked madly attractive, he thought. And suddenly the May moonlight and the enchantment of being alone with her away from etiquette—just the two of them, like any ordinary man and woman—any boy and girl—went to Dominic's head, like intoxicating wine.

He moved slowly towards her. She stood transfixed, looking up into his face. Those dark, almost tragic eyes of his were filled with an immense tenderness and longing. He put both hands on her shoulders and whispered her name:

"Catherine . . . *Catherine!*"

She could not speak, but the sweetness of that moment seemed to make an indelible mark on her life. A life that could never be the same again as she felt his arms around her, drawing her against him, and his lips on her mouth. Tenderness had become passion, longing was expressed in the warmth of that long-sustained kiss.

Also by the same author

I Should Have Known
Nightingale's Song
It Wasn't Love
Fever Of Love
Climb To The Stars
Slave Woman
Second Best
Lightning Strikes Twice
Loving And Giving
Moment Of Love
Restless Heart
Betrayal
Twice Have I Loved
The Noble One
The Snow Must Return
Never Give All
Brief Ecstasy
Desire Is Blind
Never Look Back
Infatuation
You Have Chosen
Strange Meeting
The Dark Corridor
To Love Again
Strange Rapture
Love and Desire and Hate
A Promise Is Forever
Laurence My Love
Stranger Than Fiction
(Autobiography)
Jezebel

and available in Coronet Books

A Love Like Ours

Denise Robins

CORONET BOOKS
Hodder and Stoughton

First printed in Great Britain 1969
by Hodder & Stoughton Ltd

Coronet Books edition 1972
Third impression 1979

Set, printed and bound in Great Britain for
Hodder and Stoughton Paperbacks, a
division of Hodder and Stoughton Ltd.,
Mill Road, Dunton Green, Sevenoaks, Kent,
(Editorial Office: 47 Bedford Square,
London, WC1 3DP) by Cox & Wyman Ltd., Reading

ISBN 0 340 16083 7

A LOVE LIKE OURS

1

The quiet dignity of the handsome white house in Chester Square had never seemed more attractive to Catherine Leigh-Holmes than it did today – the great day when she was home for good – looking forward to being with her father, helping to run the place for him and to entertain his friends.

She had thoroughly enjoyed the last eight months in Paris studying with one or two of her Oxford friends, perfecting her French. Before that she had taken a degree in Modern Languages at St. Anne's College and got a two-one. Not bad! But she had wanted that extra time of study and made the most of it.

Now, in her twenty-second year, she was finished with studying. Her much-loved mother had died in a tragic air disaster while Catherine was still at University, and the girl had been naturally shocked and grieved. Her father had taken his lovely wife's untimely end badly, and although he had much to occupy his mind – he was in the Diplomatic Service – Catherine knew that he was a lonely man these days. She was going to alter that. She adored her father. They were tremendous friends. She had inherited her mother's grave, special beauty, but her father's brain – his serious side – his thirst for learning. She wanted to do a serious job; perhaps in the Foreign Office. But it could wait. A year at home wouldn't matter.

The taxi-driver helped carry her cases into the hall. She paid him, shut the door, and called out:

"Daddy! Da-a-ddy! Are you in?"

He came quickly down the stairs and she greeted him rapturously, hugging and kissing him. How good-looking and distinguished he still was at the age of fifty, she thought, with that boyish figure and the silver fleck in his hair, and those clever eyes behind their horn-rimmed spectacles – eyes most unusually green which she had inherited. Her satin-smooth chestnut hair was like her mother's.

"'Home is your daughter, home from the sea,'" she misquoted, laughing.

"Home from the air would be more apt. How's Paris?" he asked.

"Just *Paris* – fabulous!" she exclaimed and shook the long brown hair back from a face usually creamy pale, now pink with excitement.

"Oh, it's good to get my lovely girl back," he said tenderly. "Come up and sit down and tell me everything. You're just in time for a sherry."

Up in the elegant double drawing-room an electric fire glowed on this cold spring evening. Mr. Leigh-Holmes thought how attractive his daughter looked in her grey skirt and white shirt, with a short green suède coat which she was fast unbuttoning with thin nervous fingers.

"Well, Daddy, are you free tonight? Are we going to be able to eat together and celebrate the Wanderer's return?"

"Yes," he nodded, "I've fixed that, Cath darling, but the day after tomorrow for quite a week, I shall be tied up because—"

She broke in:

"Never mind. I'm used to it. I'll go all-domesticated, and I can always call up one of my boy-friends." She laughed and spread her hands to the red glow of the fire.

But Edward Leigh-Holmes sighed a little as he went to the handsome Chinese lacquer cabinet which held their drinks, and poured his daughter out a sherry.

Catherine had come of age just before she got her degree. She never lacked followers. He was of an older generation yet did not disapprove of the rather motley crowd of friends who came in and out the house whenever Catherine was home. They were some of them insubordinate, untidy, long-haired and careless, but a clever lot, these young men and women of today. He envied them their vivid interest in life. The changing world was for the old a sadness—an anxiety. But for the young—a joy and a challenge.

However, he did feel it was time that his beautiful Catherine met some really nice fellow and got married. He didn't want her to wait too long.

Catherine sipped her sherry and looked round the room. It was very handsome with its long windows opening on to wrought-iron balconies—its polished floor—Adam fireplace and fine period furniture. Daddy was a connoisseur of art and they had one or two exquisite paintings.

It was a room Catherine admired, but with a discerning eye she noted that the curtains and carpet needed a good shampoo, and the Meissen birds on the glass shelves in the corner cupboard wanted a wash. Daddy had bought those when he was stationed in Bonn.

"How's our staff?" she asked suddenly.

"Fine. We're lucky. No one's left yet."

"Then we *are* lucky," she laughed, although she knew that the staff problem was always a trouble for Daddy with his pre-war standards. Because of his job and constant need to entertain, they had to be extravagant about the running of the place. The basement flat was occupied by a couple: the elderly Mrs. Anders, cook-housekeeper, and the even older Mr. Anders who acted as handy-man and butler. Other than that, there was a daily who, as Catherine often declared, produced more 'spit' than 'polish'.

Now her father was breaking it to her that she wouldn't have much time for domesticity because he needed her help.

"I've been detailed to entertain His Serene Highness Prince Dominic of Montracine," he said, "and you could be of real assistance, darling."

Her lovely eyes opened wide.

"Oh, lord, who's His Serene Highness? I forget."

In response, Mr. Leigh-Holmes picked up a glossy periodical and handed it to her.

"This might interest you."

It interested Catherine very much. Almost an entire page was devoted to the Ruler of Montracine.

How handsome he was, she thought, and remembered now having seen many photographs of him taken in various parts of Europe. She studied the fine-cut features. She liked the hint of humour about his lips. It was not a particularly strong face yet it was far from weak. The chin was obstinate and the large dark eyes compelling. A Latin type, of course, she reflected. In this particular photograph he wore State uniform.

The epaulettes on the shoulders and the rows of medals might suggest musical comedy, but somehow failed to do so. Catherine did not jeer. The Prince looked much too serious and dignified. Besides, she had seen him in other guise and knew that he was a noted sportsman. She especially recalled an account of his triumph on the Cresta Run. He was a dedicated winter-sportsman, and also played excellent polo.

She glanced down the 'Gossip Column', devoted in this issue to the Prince. There were four long paragraphs:

The twenty-five year old Prince Dominic IV of Montracine will be welcome here when he comes on his goodwill visit next week. This lucky young man is probably one of the most sought-after bachelors in Europe. Besides being the Crowned Head of a rich flourishing Principality, he is a millionaire twice over. The Crown Jewels now worn by his mother, Princesse Isabella, are worth several fortunes in themselves and await the wife whom the Prince must eventually choose. Montracine is an enchanted island and a large one, second only to Monte Cristo in size; it is situated fifty miles out in the Mediterranean facing the French and Italian Coast. For the most part the Principality is French-speaking, but there is a large Italian quarter and the Montracineans have a patois of their own.

Independence was guaranteed to Montracine (which has an area about 120 square miles), to the great-grandfather of the present Prince, who ruled as Dominic I, by Napoleon III and Garibaldi during the War of Independence which ended in 1870.

The island has a population of about 80,000 people. They export olive oil, fruit and silk. The islanders are past masters of the art of weaving glorious silks and of wood-carving.

Catherine lifted her head, having absorbed these facts, and drew breath.

"I say! Dominic must be quite something, Daddy!"

"Oh, he is, my dear. If he could only push his difficult mother more into the background, he'd be one of the best among the few ruling princes. He's a born statesman, and young though he is, he has had to deal with severe internal struggles already. But at least he can claim a guaranteed independence of his Principality which is indeed something these days. You remember the Greyharts, darling. He was our Ambassador over there before the poor chap had his first attack of angina, and they brought him back. He was dining with me at the Club last night, and reminded me that when he had lived in Montracine, he found that the Prince had a genuine and passionate desire to modernise and reform the Island completely, which was the opinion I also formed when I was over there for a short time."

"You must tell me sometime about the type of government they have on Montracine. I'd like to know," said Catherine. "Incidentally is the Prince a useful ruler?"

"Yes, indeed. When Sir Mark Daltry was over here the other day he was telling me how enormously the young man has developed. You met the Daltrys with me last summer just after Mark took over from Greyhart, didn't you?"

"Yes," Catherine nodded, "a charming rather thin little man with horn-rimmed glasses. And he has a huge tall wife – fair-haired and as jolly as a sixth-form schoolgirl, if I remember."

"Right. Daltry has plenty of brains and I don't think he'd have said much in favour of Montracine if it hadn't been true."

Catherine drew her brows together.

"Why did they send such a first-rate man as Sir Mark to a place like Montracine?"

"Make no mistake," said her father smiling, "it's becoming a very important Principality and we need a good man there."

"Tell me more about the Prince," said Catherine looking down at the intriguing face of Prince Dominic again.

"When he took over, he induced some of the big families to accept excellent reforms. For instance, he won't allow the people to be dominated by greedy landlords as they used to be, and he has built some excellent schools and first-rate hospitals. They have their own small Army because Dominic approves of military discipline. The nigger in the woodpile is Her Serene Highness. Isabella is clever and a bit of a witch. She believes that the Island would be more settled and united if the Prince got married and had a family. There has been a lot of gossip lately in the Continental papers about the Princesse trying to push him into the arms of the young daughter of his father's cousin, the Duc d'Arlennes. He's a man I can't like, and on Isabella's side. But Dominic won't consider the match. He wants to choose his own wife."

"It all sounds fascinating," said Catherine, "I'll do what I can to help but as you know, Daddy, millionaire princes aren't really my type."

"Make no mistake," said her father quickly, "Dominic is no fool. He is extremely cultured and aware of the industrial crisis in Europe. Greyhart says it was *his* idea to spend this week with bankers and industrialists, quite apart from enjoying himself. He intends to arrange for further imports to us, and it will all boost our own exports to Montracine."

Catherine picked up the magazine and looked more closely at Prince Dominic's handsome face. *Yes,* she thought, *Daddy's right. He's no fool.*

There was a lot behind those strange heavy-lidded eyes. It was the face of a dreamer, and of a thinker—definitely intriguing.

Maybe she would have to reverse her feelings about 'puppet princes' and find these next few days in the company of Prince Dominic very interesting.

2

Caroline's first meeting with the Prince was at Claridge's Hotel.

Catherine and her father arrived with Sir John and Lady Greyhart, and the aged Princesse de Palvarias, a native of Montracine who had lived in England since her husband died, just before the war. Catherine had had time before the Prince's arrival, to exchange a few words with Veronica Greyhart. She was an attractive woman, younger than her husband, still in her forties.

"You'll adore Dominic. We all call him that among ourselves," Lady Greyhart said enthusiastically, "and I'm sure he'll fall madly for you, Catherine."

"I'm sure he won't," said Catherine hastily. "He won't look at me with you around."

Veronica Greyhart smiled at the young girl affectionately.

"You're always too flattering, dear. I couldn't have got an 'A' Level if I tried when I was young. Here you are with three of them and a two-one degree in Languages. I'm sure the Prince will be most intrigued. Added to which you don't look like a bluestocking with that gorgeous figure and those big green eyes. You're much more the glamour-girl!"

Catherine protested, but Lady Greyhart laughed and turned to say a few diplomatic words to the Princesse. The old Montracinean wore black from head to foot, and leaned heavily on an ebony stick. She suffered from some obscure disease of the muscles, and lived permanently in London. She had implicit faith in English doctors.

Catherine suddenly caught sight of herself in a mirror. Yes, she thought, she would 'pass'. Shopping yesterday had been fairly successful. The new dark green dress suited her. It was short and chic, with a beaver-lamb jacket. She rarely wore a hat but for this special occasion there was a beaver-lamb cap on the side of her head. The chestnut hair was brushed smoothly to one side, and curved against her cheek.

The little reception party moved forward and stood to attention as the Prince of Montracine walked into the vestibule, followed by his private secretary; outside the staff coped with a considerable amount of luggage at the back of the magnificent Rolls that had brought the Prince from the airport. As he shook hands with Sir John and Lady Greyhart, Catherine privately wondered what he thought of Sir John whom she termed one of Daddy's 'fussy friends'. He lacked a sense of humour. Catherine was sure his own wife must sometimes find him boring. But the Prince's boyish face lit up as he turned to Edward Leigh-Holmes, and it was obvious that he had a great liking for the distinguished diplomat with his fine features, greying hair, and friendly smile.

"Ah! Good to see you again, Mr. Leigh-Holmes." The Prince held out his hand.

Leigh-Holmes bowed.

"Welcome to London, sir. May I introduce my daughter, Catherine, to Your Highness."

For the first time, Prince Dominic looked directly at the young girl. She looked at him. And for all her learning and the fact that she was used to the diplomatic world, she felt suddenly at a loss for words. She was mesmerised by the piercing glance from the Prince's large shining eyes. How very dark they were! As brilliant as agate in a fine-boned face that was well tanned by the Mediterranean sun.

He did not really look like his photograph in the magazine, she decided. It must have been taken when he was younger, and he had carried more weight. Certainly this was no self-indulgent playboy. Daddy was right—Prince Dominic was a serious young man, and most attractive. His figure was lean and graceful. All his movements were easy and swift.

He held out a hand. Catherine took it and made the smallest curtsy. She had recovered her equilibrium.

"So," he said, "this is the daughter of my good friend, Mr. Leigh-Holmes. I am delighted to meet you, Miss Leigh-Holmes."

"I am honoured, Your Highness," murmured Catherine.

His fingers felt cold. He looked pinched. No doubt he was already feeling the change of temperature. This happened to be a bitterly cold spring day and on his Island the sun must already be warming up. The countryside she thought would be golden with mimosa, and pink with almond-blossom, as was usual throughout the entire Midi.

"I remember your delightful mother," the Prince added. "She charmed us all. Her accident was a tragedy."

He had a warm attractive speaking voice. Catherine found his English excellent, with only the faintest accent. He wore very English clothes, too; a suit obviously tailored in London; a short camel's hair coat with a fur collar. He kept pulling a pair of dark glasses out of his pocket and putting them back again as though slightly nervous. She didn't think he could possibly be so, but learned later on that despite his background and education, Dominic possessed a highly-strung nervous system. He had always had to exert great strength of will in order to conquer this weakness.

"It is good of you to remember my mother, sir," murmured Catherine. She was soon to learn more about his astonishing memory. Prince Dominic must have received visits from, and entertained, a vast number of foreigners in his own country. How pleased her poor mother would have been to know that he had found her charming and memorable and regretted her death.

The Prince, still looking at Catherine, continued:

"I think I am right in saying that you were just about to go to University when your people were in Montracine. They were so proud of their clever young student."

Catherine coloured.

"I can't think why, sir," she stammered.

"I, myself, spent a year at Trinity, Oxford," he went on. "One of the happiest times of my life."

"I think most of us who have been up at Oxford remember it as a time of great happiness," she said.

"And you are now a Bachelor of Arts. What was it you read? English? Or Science, like so many young people today?"

"No, Modern Languages, sir."

"Ah! I shall test your French when we meet again."

"Please don't, sir! You terrify me!" she exclaimed, smiling.

"I am sure I do not," he said. Then moved away to speak to the old Princesse.

Now Catherine heard a flow of French exchanged between the two Montracineans.

The Prince's back was turned to her but she could still feel the extraordinary compulsion of his gaze. He did in fact alarm her, and she didn't quite know why. It certainly wasn't because she worried about her French nor was she usually embarrassed in the presence of Royalty. But the Prince of Montracine roused her interest, and made her aware of him as a *man* – that was something that didn't happen often with Catherine. She had a large number of boy-friends, but could not think of one who had produced so forceful an effect on her at first meeting.

Lady Greyhart whispered to Catherine:

"He's attractive, isn't he?"

"It seems so," said Catherine with her usual caution.

"Well, from what I've seen he couldn't take his eyes off you," said Lady Greyhart. "As John says, those green eyes of yours are really quite dangerous to any man."

Catherine coloured.

"Really, Veronica, I've never heard such nonsense," she laughed. But despite all her caution she was a little thrilled.

She now found herself involved with the Prince's private secretary. She did not take to Monsieur Henri Leveuve. He was much too smooth and he had one of those pale unhealthy faces with a blue chin, and the thread of a black moustache; typically Latin. She imagined that he was devoid of any humour but must be efficient, otherwise he wouldn't be holding such a post. He kissed Catherine's hand, discussed the English climate, then the flight from Montracine; nothing of importance. But his rather protuberant eyes which, she afterwards told her father, reminded her of a Pekinese, definitely flattered her.

"I hope we shall see more of you, Mam'selle," he murmured.

"I hope so, monsieur," she said politely, but continued to watch the slim figure of the Prince of Montracine.

The party now broke up. The royal guest was going up to his suite to wash and change while his valet unpacked. Later he was lunching with the Greyharts. He had made his own plans for this evening, Veronica whispered to Catherine. But tomorrow, there would be a special *soirée*. The old Princesse de Palvarias who had always been very social and still had a huge number of friends – some from Montracine like herself – had arranged to entertain in one of the big banqueting rooms in this hotel.

"You and your father are invited," Veronica Greyhart reminded Catherine. "It's all been rather rushed, and it means cancelling our own plans, but we've got to do it."

Really, Catherine thought, *I must be crazy but I can't stop looking at Dominic. I must be going round the bend.*

She did not expect to speak to Dominic again but he surprised her by turning around and walking back to her side. She even felt the thrill of a quickened heart-beat as he approached, giving her his warm attractive smile.

"I hear that I am to be entertained tomorrow night by my old friend Thérèse de Palvarias," he said. "You will be coming will you not, Miss Leigh-Holmes? I hope so."

That he should ask her this, and wish for her to be present, robbed her of words for a moment. She felt a fool. Her cheeks scorched with colour. She knew, too, that her lashes were flickering – a habit with her when she was embarrassed.

"I – thank you so much, sir. I – I shall be delighted and honoured."

"Do you like to dance?"

"I haven't really done much dancing, sir. There seemed so little time while I was up at Oxford, although I did go to one or two night clubs when I was in Paris."

That seemed to amuse him. He gave what Catherine thought a mischievous grin.

"Well, well! Is that the way you learned French?"

Back came her scarlet flush.

"Oh no, sir, I mean – only just during my last week – er – we went out in parties. There were several of us students living with a French family and—"

"And you found that dancing in one of those delightful

bistros to the tune of an accordion a good way of learning my language," he finished for her.

Now she had to laugh, whether it was correct to do so or not.

"How did you know that it was to *that* kind of dance I went, sir?"

"I have an idea. Believe me, I, too, have led a student's life, I miss it even now. Make no mistake, when I do go to Paris and get away from my tiresome state receptions and detectives, I head straight for some small unknown café."

She was delighted. Her heart really warmed towards him.

"Will you be able to get away from your detectives here, sir?"

"I was forced to bring one. I think I see him over there by the lift—" he grimaced. "Poor fellow! It must be such a bore for him. As much of a bore as for me to be followed. But I assure you that I intend to give him his *congé* this evening, and he will not be allowed to appear – even if disguised as a flunkey – at the party tomorrow night."

Now Catherine and the Prince laughed together. He added:

"Your father has very kindly offered to drive out of town with me tomorrow to the Hawker-Siddeley factory. One of my main objectives in coming to London this week is to meet the man who is designing a new jet aeroplane for me. My own private plane is very outdated and ready for disposal. Are you interested in flying?"

"In a way. I know nothing about it – the mechanical side, I mean – but I've done a lot of flying. Going off on holiday to so many places where my parents were stationed. I feel very sorry now that I was too young to be with Daddy when he went to all those Conferences in Montracine. I would adore to see the Island."

"Then you shall," said the Prince quickly. "I shall arrange it, personally."

Catherine drew a quick breath. She felt overwhelmed. Dominic was a very direct, decisive young man, she thought. Newspaper and magazine reports might suggest that he was in the hands of his mother, but she couldn't believe that, now she had met him. He had such an air of authority. He would go all out to achieve his own ends surely?

Now the private secretary said something to the Prince. Dominic looked at his wrist-watch and nodded.

"Good-bye for now, Miss Leigh-Holmes. I shall see you tomorrow."

"Good-bye, sir," she said. This time when she held out her hand, he kissed it.

As he walked away with his secretary, Veronica Greyhart whispered excitedly to the young girl.

"My *dear*, you seem to have made a terrific hit with His Serene Highness! As a rule he never says more than a few words to any of the girls who are introduced to him. But he seemed to be having a prolonged discussion with you."

Catherine put a nervous hand up to the collar of her dress.

"Oh, I'm sure he was just being polite."

"Not at all, and thank goodness we've found someone to amuse him," said Lady Greyhart with that warm friendly laugh that endeared her to all her friends. "I don't need to exert my charm. He finds me dull, I assure you."

The old Princesse walked slowly on her stick across to a somewhat dazed Catherine.

What a wonderful face the old woman has, the girl thought. She must have been a great beauty in her day. The ivory pale face was wrinkled but her features were still splendid and her large dark eyes most expressive.

"I am happy to think you are joining my party tomorrow night, Miss Leigh-Holmes," said the old lady. "I have met your father at many diplomatic gatherings but never had the pleasure of seeing his lovely daughter before."

"It is a pleasure to meet you also, Madame la Princesse," said Catherine.

The Princesse tapped her lightly on the shoulder with a kid-gloved hand.

"Well—well, you have made quite a success with my dear young Prince," she said.

It was the second time that she had been told this. Catherine could not help but feel flattered. The Princesse added:

"I think it is those eyes of yours, child. They are fantastic. You know Dominic said to me: 'Tell me more about this girl with the remarkable eyes. They are as green as emeralds.'"

Before Catherine could answer, an official interrupted to tell Madame la Princesse that she was wanted on the telephone. The old lady hobbled off. Catherine was left to her own rather confused thoughts.

On the way home, her father started to tell her that everybody had said that Prince Dominic admired her. Then Catherine felt suddenly irritated.

"Oh, not *you*, Daddy—*don't*! It's ridiculous. Of course he didn't admire me. He just wanted to talk to somebody and I'm not a bad conversationalist."

Mr. Leigh-Holmes put his tongue in his cheek and smiled. He knew his Catherine. Right from a child she had always been embarrassed by flattery; unlike so many other pretty girls who angled for it.

"Anyhow did *you* like *him*?" he asked her.

"I thought he was all right," said Catherine briefly, quite determined not to go into rhapsodies and cause further comment. But her father seemed anxious to know what the Prince had said to her. She told him about the new aircraft.

Mr. Leigh-Holmes nodded.

"Ah, yes, I'm taking him to Hatfield tomorrow."

"So he said."

"I have also asked him to dine at home with us one night. But why don't you drive down with us tomorrow, darling? I'm sure he wouldn't mind."

There was nothing that Catherine would rather have done, but some kind of reluctance to appear too eager, prompted her to make an excuse, and refuse the tempting offer.

"Sorry, Daddy, I shall be busy. I have got several things to do before the *soirée* tomorrow night."

"A pity."

They chatted together like the great friends they were until they reached Chester Square, after which Mr. Leigh-Holmes had to rush off to keep an appointment, and Catherine went up to her room.

3

The enchantment of the Princesse de Palvarias's supper-dance was to make Catherine feel she was more than mortal. She felt touched by a magic she had never experienced before.

There seemed no room for memories of University, Paris, student life, all the hundred and one facets of a modern girl's life. She found that she was neither sophisticated nor blasé, but utterly thrilled.

When the Leigh-Holmes arrived, a great many guests were already present in the reception room. They moved down a queue towards their hostess – the old Princesse – who was exquisite in black lace, with a Spanish lace mantilla over her head. Beside her stood the Guest of Honour – the Prince of Montracine.

Lights sparkled from the huge crystal chandeliers. An orchestra played soft background music. The room was elegant and romantic with gay banks of spring flowers and hot-house plants everywhere. The guests, in full evening dress, talked together in groups but all heads turned to watch the newcomers being 'received'.

The entrance of Catherine Leigh-Holmes followed by her distinguished father, caused a slight stir. Those in the Foreign Office who knew Edward Leigh-Holmes seemed a little startled by the sight of Catherine. She was remembered for the most part as an attractive but ordinary sort of young girl with a studious mind. But one of the elderly diplomats remarked to his wife tonight:

"I didn't know Leigh-Holmes had such a stunning daughter."

Catherine was well aware her tight-fitting emerald satin dress, worn with her mother's splendid jewellery, was a success. Her father had already told her that she looked positively staggering. The chestnut hair brushed high off her forehead, with those two rich curls brushing the creamy pallor of one cheek, was more than effective.

She wore long green satin gloves. The golden brown mink stole over one arm, was another legacy from her mother.

"What a beautiful dress, my child," murmured the Princesse.

Catherine thanked her, moved on and made her small graceful curtsy to His Serene Highness. As she straightened, Prince Dominic looked down into the girl's magnificent eyes and with the faintest grin, which put her completely at ease, whispered:

"Did you find the dress to match the eyes or put emerald drops into those eyes, to match the dress?"

She bit hard on her lips in order not to giggle. She must at all cost retain her dignity. But her heart beat quite wildly as he added:

"After supper, remember, please, the first dance with me."

"Thank you, sir."

She managed to say the words with a coolness she was far from feeling. She moved on and greeted Henri Leveuve and one or two other people she knew, then made a bee-line for Veronica Greyhart who wore pearl-grey chiffon and her famous pearls, and was, Catherine thought, outstanding.

Lady Greyhart on her part gazed enviously at the young girl.

"Honestly, it's not fair, Catherine. You make us all look so ordinary."

"Dear Veronica, you're always good for my ego and I don't believe a word of it."

"I think it's going to be rather a gay affair. Everybody who is anybody has come. Dominic is a great favourite and he always picks up friends and admirers wherever he goes."

Catherine, whose heart-beats were quietening down, took a glass of champagne from the tray handed to her by a waiter and sipped it thirstily. It was hot in here. She would go and leave her stole in the powder room. It had been foolish to bring it. Veronica, always talkative, chatted to her but Catherine's gaze kept wandering to the tall slim graceful figure of the young prince. Like the other men he wore white-tie-and-tails with a small white carnation in his buttonhole. In the glittering lights his ebon-black hair looked like satin, she thought, and against the very white collar and shirt, his skin was gorgeously brown. How handsome he was! *How very princely*. Yet mustn't he be bored, having to talk to all these people whom he knew only vaguely and perhaps did not meet from one year's end to another? Wasn't the burden of etiquette thrown upon the shoulders of people in his position almost unbearable?

She could not think of him tonight as a prince seriously governing his Island. Only as the young man who had stood beside her yesterday, telling her about his sports-car, and about his sailing, and how he preferred to go out on that blue Mediterranean sea with special friends in a small boat, rather than in his handsome yacht with a large crew surrounded by people, facing, inevitably, a battery of cameras.

He was really very human and perhaps the strange melancholy which she read in his dark thickly-lashed eyes, sprang from an inner yearning for the freedom he could never really have.

Now another ripple of excitement went through the crowd of guests. There was a lull in the buzz of conversation. The sound of the orchestra could be heard more clearly.

Catherine saw that they were all watching the arrival of the Birninghams with their model-girl daughter and her brother, Rupert. Nobody looked at Rupert, but everybody certainly looked at Louise. She moved, Catherine thought, with professional grace and languor. Extremely tall and thin, she wore a breathtaking dress of white silk crêpe moulded to her glorious figure; one shoulder bare. Over the other there floated a long scarf of sapphire-coloured chiffon. Long sapphire-blue gloves completed the effect. Her skin was almost as white as the dress and her blonde hair smoothed tightly over her small skull and coiled in a huge chignon at the back. Long sapphire and diamond earrings shivered and gleamed as she walked.

Catherine, with a strange intensity, watched the Prince receive this marvellous-looking girl. Catherine was near enough to note with genuine surprise that he gave Louise only a polite smile, said a few words, then turned to the next guest.

Feeling absurdly pleased, remembering how much longer he had smiled and spoken to *her*, Catherine drank some more of her champagne and moved away with her father to talk to friends.

She had been so sure that the Prince would be struck by lightning when he saw the fabulous Louise. She felt madly excited at the thought of that first dance after supper.

The next two hours seemed to her long and meaningless. Plenty of conversation—plenty of flattery from other young men—and an excellent dinner in the banqueting hall.

But she had been seated far down at the end of the table a long way away from the hostess and her glamorous Guest of Honour.

Catherine was near enough to Louise Birningham, however, to see her giving the two men on either side of her the full benefit of her blue-lidded eyes and long false lashes. But Louise didn't seem to be saying much. Catherine, herself, felt less like talking than usual. She was normally an enthusiastic conversationalist. But she felt tonight that there was something strange and compelling on her mind – absorbing her – reducing her to silence.

She did not really do justice to the excellent supper: turtle soup, *délice de Sole* (the Prince liked Dover sole because it was a fish that did not care for the warm waters of the Mediterranean and was for him a delicacy). English saddle of lamb, and a mountainous meringue and strawberry sweet, with choice of gateaux, followed by coffee and liqueurs. It seemed to Catherine an endless meal. At last the Princesse rose and the Prince followed suit. All the guests turned to watch as the two walked through to the banqueting hall. Footmen had thrown open the double doors. The sound of dance music from the other room reached them plainly now.

Then and then only, did Catherine feel that she came to life. As Prince Dominic passed her, he turned his head and gave her a long look – an almost imperceptible nod as though to remind her that this was the time for dancing.

Her throat felt dry. She rubbed her fingers together and asked herself chaotically whether she ought to go to him, or wait for him to return to her. Lady Greyhart propelled her forward.

"Come along – let's powder our noses."

In the powder room, Catherine dusted her small straight nose with a puff, and straightened a rich curl of hair that had fallen out of place. She looked into the mirror, hardly recognising the excitement in her own sparkling eyes. She so rarely felt excited in quite this way. She was suddenly panic-stricken. She wanted to rush out of the hotel and hide at home . . . she could not dance with the Prince . . . she had lost her nerve.

In a chaotic frame of mind she decided, however, to re-enter the reception room with Veronica. The Prince stood near the doorway. He was laughing at a remark Thérèse de Palvarias had just made. She was a witty old lady.

Dominic turned. He saw the young girl in green. He moved at once towards her.

"I have been telling the Princesse that my first dance is with you, Miss Leigh-Holmes."

She wished rather stupidly, that she could ask him to call her 'Catherine'. That surname sounded so stiff, so formal.

"It was an excellent supper," went on Prince Dominic, "I must admit I enjoy my food and such excellent English lamb especially."

More at ease, she said:

"So do I, sir."

"No formalities," he reminded her, put an arm around her, took her gloved hand in his and steered her on to the floor.

He danced like a dream, she thought, her heart beating fast. Of course in his position he must be very accustomed to diplomatic balls. He moved with the natural grace and rhythm of the Latin. It was truly dancing in the old-fashioned way rather than the modern. But Catherine found it fascinating.

She seemed to move on winged feet across the polished floor. And she felt a feminine thrill of vanity, and pleasure because she knew that many other women were watching enviously; perhaps some of the older ones were annoyed because the Prince had not danced first of all with them. He was certainly a rebel tonight, cutting loose from etiquette.

I don't care, Catherine thought, her self-confidence reviving, *I don't care if they're all muttering oaths and all furious with me.*

Tall though she was, the Prince was at least a head taller. The top of her burnished head only touched his chin. He murmured:

"Please allow me to say that you look very lovely tonight."

"It's k-kind of you . . ." she only just managed not to add the 'sir'.

"And you told me you do not do much dancing. But you are wonderful."

"You flatter me."

"I try never to flatter people. I tell them the truth," he said seriously. "I have danced with some of the most perfect dancers, some of the most beautiful women in Europe. I know exactly what attracts me and what does not."

I know too, thought Catherine, and closed her eyes tightly. She did not dare look up into her partner's intriguing face. He went on dancing, murmuring in her ear:

"This visit to London is turning out well – a wonderful break for me. I did not expect to enjoy myself so much."

"Oh, I'm glad that you're enjoying it!" she exclaimed.

He looked down at her with a searching gaze which she found unnerving.

"When your cheeks grow warm," he said, "it is not like an ordinary blush, but a warm glow spreading suddenly through the petals of a camellia."

Catherine gasped.

"The Prince of Montracine is a poet," she said.

"Yes, I am quite fond of poetry and I write it when I have time," was his unexpected answer.

Feeling more at ease now, she talked to him about poetry

as they went on dancing. The band was playing an old favourite now—"*The Green Fields of Summer*". It was in slower tempo than the one before. A little sad and nostalgic, Catherine felt the Prince's arm pull her a trifle closer.

"Do *you* by any chance write poetry?" he asked.

"I used to when I was at University, but I don't let anybody see it."

"I would like to see what you write and learn what your thoughts are, Catherine. Please show me something you have written."

"Oh, I couldn't possibly," she protested and laughed.

"I insist!"

"Is that a royal command?" she asked mischievously.

Now he broke right through the restraining ropes of protocol and gave her the smallest shake.

"You mock me! Ridiculous girl, I never give royal commands. You have been reading too many romantic books about autocratic European rulers."

Oh, thought Catherine, *he's marvellous. He's so human.*

Dominic set her senses swimming again by leaning his head down and whispering:

"You are the most unbelievably attractive woman I have ever met."

The music ended. The dancers stood still, and clapped for more. Dominic said, regretfully:

"I must leave you now and ask some of the other women to dance and try to behave myself. But I will come back."

Catherine stood speechless—breathless. She felt lost. She didn't know where she was or what to say or do. She was quite shaken. But as they walked across the room towards her father, Dominic added:

"I will do my duty dances then come back to you, you lovely ridiculous girl, so await the royal command."

"Oh!" she gasped, her cheeks on fire.

He gave her no time to say more, but bowed, heels together, and after a brief word with her father, left them.

The memory of the expression in his eyes, half-tender, half-mocking, haunted her for the rest of the evening. But he did not come back.

Perhaps because he found it too difficult, he did not invite her to dance with him again.

4

When Catherine woke up that next morning it was to a new day of unexpected happiness.

She had gone to bed in a rather sad and disappointed state of mind, wondering if she had said or done the wrong thing with the Prince last night because he had seemed so studiously to avoid her during the rest of the evening. She went over and over again in her mind every little thing that he had said, and that she had said in turn. She re-lived every moment of that fabulous dance that had made her feel she was held suspended in space rather than being guided across the floor of a conventional ballroom.

Finally she decided that the Prince of Montracine was utterly charming, but, like a thousand other men, he found it agreeable to be flattering with a young girl. And just why he had chosen her for that first dance, instead of the gorgeous Louise Birningham – well, that to Catherine remained inexplicable.

I don't suppose I'll ever see him again, she had thought just before falling into an exhausted sleep.

That next morning she went downstairs in her dressing-gown to get some coffee and see how her father was. She found him gone. It was past ten o'clock. She had slept late. Then Mrs. Anders came up from the basement with a note for her.

While Catherine waited for her coffee, she read it, yawning, still drowsy-eyed. She was crestfallen to discover that

Daddy had had an urgent call from one of his superiors and at this very time was at London Airport waiting to fly to the Lebanon. He would be away, he said, for three days at least.

> "*I couldn't get out of it, darling,*" he ended the note, "*although I am supposed to be playing host-in-chief to Montracine. But they have apparently told him that this is an emergency. They've asked Greyhart to look after him for me. I expect he'll be gone by the time I get back...*"

Now Catherine's spirits fell slowly but surely. With an important diplomat for a father, one had to get used to the sudden departures and alterations in plan, but she had a sinking feeling that this would be the end of the magic she had so unexpectedly found with Prince Dominic. The very fact that she had always prided herself on being emotionally controlled – rather cool and cautious in her dealing with the opposite sex – intensified her belief that she had let her thoughts circle far too freely and intensely around the Prince. She hoped she had behaved circumspectly but she had to admit that she felt an extraordinary excitement while she was with him and when he had looked so searchingly down into her eyes.

Of course she had been a fool, she thought sadly. She need not expect to be allowed to see much more of the Prince. That privilege would be Veronica Greyhart's. But Catherine was totally unprepared for what happened next to put her disappointment right into reverse.

She had hardly finished dressing and tidying the room before Mrs. Anders called up to her:

"Miss – Miss – a gentleman's just left a letter for you."

She ran downstairs. She took the envelope and turned it over, she saw that the crest was that of Claridge's Hotel.

With a fast-beating heart she took it up to her room again. She sat down on the bed and opened the letter. She did not recognise the handwriting which was firm and bold. Before reading the contents she looked at the signature and at once her whole body seemed to pulsate with life and that unaccustomed sense of excitement which she had only just been deploring.

It was from him.

"*My dear Catherine,*

My old friend the Princesse gave me a wonderful party. I thoroughly enjoyed last night. The outstanding part was my dance with you. I was sorry my various commitments did not allow me to repeat it. I looked for you when it all ended, but you and your father had gone.

As I am in London only semi-officially, I can please myself a little and if you really meant your kind invitation to dine quietly with you at your home, I would like very much to do so, tomorrow night.

I will telephone you at about half past ten . . .

Yours most sincerely,

Montracine."

Catherine lifted her eyes from this note. So she *hadn't* done the wrong thing or blotted her copybook last night. She was surprised and elated that Dominic should have taken the trouble to have written to her like this. She could imagine Tom, her favourite student friend might have thought her a snob—flattered, because Dominic was a famous person—a ruling Prince. But it wasn't true. It was the man himself who fascinated her and it would have been all the same to her if he had been an ordinary person in an ordinary job. She just wanted to see *him* again. The man, not the Prince.

Her feelings fluctuated once more as she remembered that her father had gone away so she couldn't ask the Prince to dinner. Although there was precious little convention left in this day and age, she was still Edward Leigh-Holmes's daughter and must preserve some of the diplomatic traditions.

Oh, she thought, *now what can I do?*

She knew perfectly well that Dominic did not want a formal party; that was the sort of thing he was trying to get away from.

She sat reading his letter over and over again until the telephone bell rang and scattered her wits. This must be *him.* What on earth was she to say? Wouldn't she be wise just to appear indifferent, apologise politely, and explain that she could not now invite him to her home because her father had been called away? But once she heard that attractive voice, with its faint accent, any ideas of appearing disinterested vanished. Dominic said:

"Good-morning, Catherine, I trust you are not too tired. I saw you being besieged for many dances."

"Oh . . . No – I – I w-wasn't, really," she stammered.

"You got my note?"

"Yes, thank you, sir."

"We agreed you should drop this mode of address."

"Thank you, D-Dominic," she continued to stutter, and inwardly prayed for a return to her normal control. She seemed to be losing it.

"I did not know you stuttered, Catherine."

She detected the teasing note in his voice.

"I – I—" she began, then stopped and began to laugh helplessly.

"Catherine," he said. "May I come along and sample your cooking?"

"I'm so terribly sorry, but my father has left town. He had an urgent call, early this morning, and is on his way to Beirut. Perhaps you haven't heard, but I know how very disappointed he was to have to cut short this week with you in London. I expect Sir John will be ringing you – I know he and Lady Greyhart will do their best to entertain you," she ended lamely.

He said:

"That is bad news for me. The Greyharts are sweet people but I have always had the warmest and most friendly feelings towards your father. And now that I have met his daughter—" the Prince broke off significantly.

Catherine began to feel acutely nervous. She was forced to realise that she was not nearly so sophisticated – as much of a woman of the world as she had imagined. She found herself reduced to a state of schoolgirl confusion. Only one thing stood out clearly and that was that if it was going to be made impossible for her to see more of the Prince she would never get over it.

Never get over it. More schoolgirl exaggeration. What *was* the matter with Catherine Leigh-Holmes? she wondered in dismay.

There was a moment of silence and she half-feared that Dominic was no longer at the other end of the line. Then he spoke again.

"Well, look, this being so, and if we are both so fettered by conventional propriety – I have a plan. I am afraid I still intend to be a rebel for a few days. Will you join with me, Catherine?"

"Of course," she said with a breathless laugh. "I've always had an admiration for rebels."

"Then I suggest that I give my detective and my secretary the slip tomorrow night and creep out of the hotel, and that you join me in some quite unheard of little restaurant in a back street and we dine together. I can be Mr. Smith and you can be Miss Jones."

Excitement grew in her and she warmed to this proposal. "It sounds terrific. But do you really think —"

"I do not intend to think," he broke in, "I just intend to do what I want for a change, and I wish to spend a very happy evening with you, quite regardless of either my position or yours. You know your capital better than I do, where would you suggest that we eat, Miss Jones?"

"I shall have to think, Mr. Smith," she laughed, taking her cue from him.

"Catherine, you are a darling," he said suddenly. "Well, you suggest the place, and I will leave it to you to book the table – in the name of Mr. Smith, please. Send me a note at my hotel tomorrow afternoon, marked 'Strictly Private', and after a busy day of duty-calls, I will join you – say at eight o'clock, or pick you up at your home. I will come in a taxi."

"I shall be plainly dressed and wear a headscarf," she said.

"I am sure you will look delightful, although when I have thoughts of you, you will always be in the emerald-green dress that matches your eyes."

Now he was deliberately flirting with her, she thought, and the feeling of panic came back. But he gave her no time to say more.

"Till tomorrow night then, Miss Jones."

"Till tomorrow, Mr. Smith," she returned.

When she put the receiver down, her cheeks felt so hot that she had to sit there, fanning herself. She felt as though she were taking part in a marvellous fictitious intrigue – play-acting – stepping out of the pages of some historical romance. For whatever slant one might put upon this meeting with Prince Dominic, to her it held the very essence of romance. Something she had never come up against in her life before. She had to admit that she was dazzled. In every girl alive there is a romantic side, no matter how hard she might try to subdue it, or present a more realistic and cynical attitude towards the world. However ridiculous it was, this secret meeting between 'Mr. Smith' and 'Miss Jones' was the most exciting thing that had ever happened to Catherine. She was well aware that he was trying to get away from the affairs of his country and the many inflexible cords that bound him to it. He wanted, rather pathetically, perhaps, to become the young student he used to be over here. To be *himself*. And he had chosen her to share the experience.

Of course, Catherine thought, *I am crazy to let it affect me. It will be a lot of fun for him and then he'll go back to his Island and forget that 'Miss Jones' ever existed.*

Later on she told Mrs. Anders that she would be out for dinner tomorrow evening. She then thought about various restaurants she had been to and tried to make up her mind which one to choose for Dominic. It mustn't be too smart or well-known. She must make sure that it was the sort of place none of her friends, or the Prince's, would patronise; yet the food must be good.

Suddenly she remembered a conversation she had had with her cousin, Belinda Holt – Catherine was godmother to one of Belinda's twins. They often met. Belinda had told her that she and her husband, James, recently tried out Sacchoni's – a small Italian restaurant just opened in George Street. The food was gorgeous. But too expensive for James. So Belinda was not likely to go there again.

Catherine was sure Dominic wouldn't mind Italian cooking. He had Italian blood in him.

Catherine, herself, went over to see this place – *Sacchoni's* – and reserve a table. She found it as Belinda said, small and rather crowded, and it didn't look at all smart. She was quite sure she and the Prince would meet nobody they knew there.

The feeling of excitement grew stronger as Catherine went home and wrote to Dominic. She addressed the envelope with great formality. But her note was the reverse:

"*Dear Mr. Smith,*

If you would fetch me tomorrow in a taxi at ten to eight I will be waiting at the corner of my side of the Square, wearing a camel hair coat and green headscarf. If it's raining I shall have an umbrella.

Yours in haste,

Miss Jones."

As she licked the flap of the envelope she giggled to herself.

The next evening she was waiting at the end of the Square just before the time indicated. She half expected that the Prince by now might have regretted his part in this intrigue and wouldn't turn up. But of course he did, and promptly, too. As his taxi drew up at the kerb she felt the craziest joy. She admonished herself.

Don't be too idiotic, Catherine, or you'll be sorry.

The Prince did not get out of the taxi but put out a hand and drew her on to the seat beside him. She felt glad of the sudden shelter from the wind and savoured the rich aroma of the cigar which he had obviously been smoking.

As they passed the flashing lights in the streets, she could see his brown handsome face smiling at her. He wore the short coat with the beaver collar in which she had first seen him. His eyes were shining. He raised her hand to his lips then let it fall.

"Punctuality is a most admirable trait in a woman and, I am told, a rare one," he said. "Thank you for waiting for me, Catherine – I mean Miss Jones."

"Thank you for being on time, Mr. Smith."

"It is so cold . . ." he gave a little shiver. "After my Mediterranean sun, I find your climate a little too gloomy perhaps, but oh, how I love it! How I love this taxi instead of my Rolls. And how I love being with you, Miss Jones, instead of many of the tiresome ladies I have to entertain."

"I can be tiresome, too," Catherine said with a laugh.

"I have seen no signs of it so far. Would you like a cigarette?"

"Not just now."

He stretched out his long legs and sighed.

"I really do feel as though a gate has been unlocked and I have been liberated."

"Do you live in a sort of prison, really?"

"A beautiful one and I am devoted to my gaolers, my Island, my people, my good friends. But even in 1969 it is impossible for a man in my position to get away very often and do exactly as he wishes."

Catherine had grown used to admiration. She had her many followers. But tonight she felt an unusual sense of privilege because *she*, Catherine Leigh-Holmes, had been chosen to share this evening of stolen freedom with Dominic. She wanted to say so, but felt tongue-tied. When she turned her head to look at him, he was looking straight down at her with his big expressive eyes. She felt almost uncomfortable because of the degree of warmth and feeling in those eyes, but she pretended to be blind to it.

"I do hope you'll like this little restaurant," she said. "It was recommended to me. It's right the other side of the Park. I'm sure we won't meet anybody we know there."

"Excellent."

They turned into the Park and moved along with the traffic towards Marble Arch. Dominic commented on the strange sight of the Hilton Hotel – so high, so modernistic – towering above the beautiful old period houses in Park Lane. *Little* houses now, but when he was a boy in London before the Hilton had been built, they had seemed so tall.

"I have no real liking for modern architecture," he said. Catherine agreed with him.

"I hate all these skyscrapers."

"I am so glad to hear you say so. You will not then be disappointed in my Island. We have no skyscrapers. I, personally, supervise the planning of all new buildings and am what the English call 'a headache' to the architects' progressive ideas. So many of our beautiful buildings are two and three hundred years old, like my palace, which is small but has all the elegance and charm of the eighteenth century. My mother has more advanced tastes. She thinks that I should surrender my artistic feelings and allow a more modern note to creep in. Of course she is right, so far as the advancement of our people is concerned. I concede to modern architecture for our industrial buildings. But I will not have great square hotels built of steel and concrete, with their soul-destroying glass façades. I insist that even our best and biggest shops have to be of a design to fit in with the beauty of the hills and terraces and the older buildings."

"It all sounds super!" exclaimed Catherine. "I shall love it. And surely Montracine must be a great attraction to tourists. These new monstrosities have no individuality. I think you are right to veto them."

"You must say so to my mother, and my First Minister of State, Monsieur de Reynard."

"Reynard," repeated Catherine. "*The Fox!*"

"A good name for him, perhaps. He is a wily man, and in my mother's opinion, responsible for the successful administration of my Island. Although of course . . ." he laughed lightly, "I like to think *I* am responsible."

Catherine sat silent. She noticed how often he spoke of his mother and remembered her father telling her that Dominic was no 'puppet Prince', and that Her Serene Highness, the Princesse Isabella, was trying to put too much pressure on him.

5

They talked animatedly until they reached the little Italian restaurant which Dominic at once found amusing and entirely suitable for the occasion. He laughed at Catherine and sniffed the air delightedly.

"This aroma of garlic and oil and herbs and the sight of the onions hanging up with the fat sausages, and all those rows of Chianti bottles make me think I am looking through the windows of one of the cafés on my own Island where I am never allowed to eat. How sick I get of grandeur and the ceremonies which befit my position. This is glorious. You have chosen well, Catherine."

She was relieved. She had been half afraid he would find *Sacchoni's* beneath his dignity. But she might have known that it was what he wanted – mainly to forget that he was one of the Crowned Heads of Europe. Yet he would never really lose his dignity, she thought. He stood out among all the other men in the restaurant. He really had a wonderful face, a distinguished bearing which would always single him out from ordinary men.

He at once won the heart of the Italian who owned *Sacchoni's*. The Signor rubbed his hands delightedly together when addressed in his own language so perfectly spoken, gave them a corner table apart from the crowd, and set to work to recommend his best dishes.

In all her life Catherine had never enjoyed anything more than that meal. Pasta – veal with mushrooms – creamy cheese. *And* Dominic's company. She felt once more touched by the magic the Prince of Montracine cast over her. She was delighted, too, because Dominic seemed also to enjoy the food and wine and kept saying what fun it all was.

"If poor old Leveuve could see me here like this – his eyes would pop out of his head!"

"They're not very nice eyes, so I wouldn't mind if they did," said Catherine, then blushed and said she was sorry for being rude about his private secretary. Dominic laughed.

"I agree with you. He has rather horrid eyes like huge marbles, but he is a clever one. My mother trusts him absolutely, and, so really, do I. Although sometimes I think he spies on me."

How awful, Catherine thought, to be spied upon. To be in a position where so many searchlights were constantly focused upon you.

He was always quoting his mother; somehow Catherine did not think she would care for the Italian-born Dowager Princesse. But now her thoughts were re-directed upon the man opposite her. He raised his glass.

"To this hour of freedom, shared with the most beautiful girl I have ever seen."

"That is surely an exaggeration."

"Not in my opinion. Once when I was a boy I travelled to Finland with my father. I remember a lake there, and it was purest green. Your eyes are as clear and green as that lake, Catherine."

She could think of nothing to say. She shook her head.

"Catherine," he went on, "it is difficult for me to express the depth of my pleasure in this new friendship I have found with you. I assure you I am not idly flattering. I meet many women and I have formed one or two friendships with French and Italian girls in my own country. But they have meant little. As you know, I am very pro-English and I have the greatest admiration for English women – for their sincerity, their direct and frank approach to life, their sportsmanship. You have all these attributes combined with great beauty, and that is rare."

"You're awfully kind," murmured Catherine and sat there tongue-tied, confused, wanting to treat his praise lightly but unable to do so. She had lost her usual poise.

He raised his glass to her again:

"To the wonderful eyes of my new friend."

His reiterance of the word 'friend' steadied her. This time she returned the toast warmly:

"And to my new and very first Montracinean friend."

"Catherine," he went on, "I was thinking last night that you told me you write poetry."

"*Used* to write it," she corrected him, "but it was a phase I got over. You also said you were a poet."

"Yes, but even if I do not write it now, I still read a lot of it in many languages."

"Tell me about something *you* have written," she said, while the waiter cleared the table and brought them strong black coffee.

"One day perhaps, but only on condition you return the compliment."

Catherine sat back in her chair. With her long slender fingers she twirled the stem of her wine glass. The man opposite stared at her as though fascinated. Two nights ago he had thought her disturbingly lovely in her evening dress. He liked her just as much in the short grey-wool knitted dress with the polo-collar which she wore tonight. It clung to the slim lines of her body and moulded the perfection of her small pointed breasts. She had put on long gold earrings and a matching bracelet.

The more closely he studied Catherine Leigh-Holmes the more he learned about the details of that face which had haunted him from the first moment he saw it. He could even be entranced by her imperfections; the dark mole on the creamy pallor of one cheek; a slight irregularity of teeth, eyebrows perhaps a little too heavily marked, yet he was thankful she did not pluck them into ridiculous crescents, or the sort of pencil-line that made masks of many girls instead of faces. There was something so natural about Catherine, especially the way she blushed. He was entranced when that bright pink surged into her cheeks.

After a moment she said:

"You may not believe this but I was rather a solitary sort of child. I always longed to have a brother or sister but didn't, and being the only one, and with Daddy always busy, having to rush away, and poor Mummy going with him, I spent a lot of time away from my parents and home. They didn't realise it of course, but I would have given anything in the world to have had a greater sense of security and more family life. Perhaps that is why I poured my heart out into my poems. Can you understand that?"

"Very well, because I was the same. Not because my parents were ever away for long, but because as a small boy I was brought up in a palace to be the future ruler of a great little Island, and felt very solitary—and even insecure like yourself. Always alone in a crowd—but never really alone. That was the difference between us as children perhaps, but the effect is equally distressful. Such a child begins to draw into a shell and live within himself. Not that you give the slightest sign now that you were once like this."

"Years of boarding-school, then University, knocked a lot of the nonsense out of me," she laughed.

"I still suffer from the 'nonsense'," he smiled and sighed.

"Well, I think a person like yourself must have had more cause for being introspective. But *you* don't show what *you* must have suffered."

"Oh, yes, I do – frequently," he laughed, then went on: "Try to remember just one verse that you wrote when you were about fourteen or fifteen, Catherine. That's the age when one writes down one's heart, is not it?"

She nodded and searched her mind, then a little shyly said:

"I was once taken by an aunt down to the sea in Cornwall while my parents were in Australia. It was, as you say, when I was in my early teens. They thought I would like it on the Cornish coast but the wild winds and the cruel rocks affected me. I used to lie awake and cry about nothing. It was stupid. But then the very young do feel sort of tragic at times . . ." she gave a little laugh . . . "I never showed the poems to anybody, of course, but I remember this one:

'I would the sea were quieter
For at night I cannot sleep.
The waves keep moaning, sobbing,
Till I feel that I must weep.
I lie here in the darkness
And my eyelids burn and smart
For the sea's perpetual crying
Seems to break my very heart.'

I expect you'll laugh at that," she hastily added.

But Dominic's face looked intent and serious.

"Oh, but I do not – I could not. It's a beautiful little poem even though so sad. I understand. We have terrible storms over our Island and as a boy I also used to lie awake and listen and pull the blanket over my head. Not because I was physically afraid but because, like you, the awful sadness of the wild gales can be heartbreaking. Please quote me something more that you have written."

"No, I couldn't. I don't remember anything more," she

shook her head vigorously and added: "You are the only one who has ever heard a line I have written. I have been too afraid of being laughed at."

"That is very English. The English are afraid of emotion. I am Latin and more extrovert – these days, anyhow."

She looked at him, fascinated.

What a strange mixture he was – this young Prince who had the soul of a poet. Yet he could never be accused of being effeminate.

She said:

"Look – you've cheated. I want to hear one of *your* poems."

"I have no memory and I have not looked for years at my own work. But when you come to Montracine I will unearth some, I promise."

"Shall I ever come to Montracine, do you think?"

"Yes," he said, "you must. I would not care to go away and feel I was never going to see you again, Catherine."

This time he put out a hand and took one of hers and pressed it in a strong nervous clasp. It was the first time there had been such direct physical contact between them, for that handclasp could be called anything but light or formal, and the expression in his eyes was of the utmost seriousness. It stunned Catherine. She felt the strength ebb from her. She could not even draw her fingers away, nor her gaze from his. It was as though she were mesmerised. Then, as an anticlimax, their little waiter bustled up and asked the Signor if he would like more coffee.

Dominic released her hand and sat back in his chair.

"*Si, si,*" he said abruptly. He pulled out a handkerchief and dabbed his forehead. "It is hot in here," he muttered.

She found her breath.

"Yes, it is."

He made her look at him again.

"You *will* come to Montracine. I shall ask your father when he is next due some leave, or even if you come only for a long week-end, but you *must* see my Island. I will send my own plane for you. It will not be the new one but my old friend will bring you to the Island – whenever you wish."

A dazed Catherine said:

"Thank you – thank you very much."

"And in case I do not see you again before I leave London, I would like you to have my own telephone number – the direct line to my private rooms in the Palace."

He drew a notebook from his pocket, tore out a page, and with a gold pencil scribbled a number and handed it to her.

"At any time of the day or night if you ask for this, you can reach me," he said.

"Thank you," she said again breathlessly, feeling it to be a weak and inadequate reply, and feeling, too, that she was in some kind of fantastic dream from which she must soon awaken.

But one thing hit her with considerable force: that for her this was no mere passing enchantment. This extraordinary young man had touched the very depths of her heart.

When the evening ended, she knew that she was in love – hopelessly of course, for how could it be anything but hopeless between two people in such different worlds? But in love she was, and for the first time in her life. And that slip of paper with his private telephone number – a number which surely he must give to very few people in the world – was more precious to her than had he placed the finest diamond inside her bag.

6

In her private writing-room, Her Serene Highness, Princesse Isabella of Montracine sat writing a very private and personal letter to her great friend and lifelong admirer, the Duc d'Arlennes, who was a resident of the Island.

She had just spent an hour talking to her son's secretary, Henri Leveuve. He came more often than the Prince ever knew for the sort of discussion that he and the Princesse had had this morning. They were skilfully manœuvred talks on both sides, with Isabella probing into her son's affairs and the private secretary passing on information in a manner which might have been considered almost treasonable had it not been that Her Serene Highness asked the questions. Henri Leveuve was a subtle man with a dangerous wit and perception and a traitorous nature, well-concealed behind an apparent affection and friendship for his master.

Everything that he passed on to the Princesse in the way of information, he managed to excuse to himself on the grounds that it was for 'His Highness's good'; besides which Isabella was a powerful woman – a power to the Ministers who gathered around her and a foe to those who tried, she well knew, to push her more into the background. She had always influenced her husband while he was alive and she had no intention of handing the reins entirely over to her son now that he was on the throne.

Anybody who could see the Princesse on this golden morning of the Mediterranean spring in the beautiful panelled room with its exquisite furniture and priceless paintings, might have been impressed by the sight of that queenly form seated at the satinwood bureau. She held an old-fashioned purple-feathered quill between her long thin fingers – she despised modern pens – and wrote rapidly in a delicate slanting Italian hand. At fifty-five she was still a beautiful woman, her jet-black hair dressed in Italian style high on her head. For most of the time she wore dark colours and none of the fashion houses from Paris or Rome had yet been able to dissuade her from the long flowing skirts which she favoured. She had always been proud of her small waist. It was clasped today by a wide gold belt, matching the heavy gold necklace wound three times around her long throat.

When she lifted her head for a moment and closed her eyes as though thinking, an artist might well marvel at the sculptured beauty of Isabella's pale face, spoiled only by the thinness of her lips. It was a magnificent if hard face. But those brilliant eyes could flash fire when she was roused, and she was a person whom people either adored or feared. She was adept at hiding a great deal of her power-lust under a cloak of feminine sweetness. It was said of her that when Isabella of Montracine was at her most charming, she was most dangerous.

Now she stood up and walked to one of the tall windows that opened on to a wide balcony with a white and scarlet awning.

Letter in hand, she stared down at the land she knew so well, the beautiful well-cared-for gardens, laid out in terraces overlooking the sea. The blue sea glittered, diamond-bright, in the early sunshine. A wonderful morning and she was glad that Dominic was back. She did not like it when he was not here, neither did she share his affection for England and the English people. Expressly she disliked it when he was out of the control that she liked to feel she could still exert over him.

She had seen him only for a brief hour last night when he returned, but he had seemed fatigued, and retired early, unwilling to talk a great deal. The only time he had expanded was when he had described his visit to the Hawker-Siddeley factory and the new, beautiful aircraft he had ordered.

He had seemed quite unusually *distrait*, which Isabella had at once noticed, she suspected that her son had been 'up to something' that he did not want to reveal to her. It was only after her talk with Leveuve that she knew.

He had fallen in love.

Leveuve had not actually said so but he had inferred as much, and the inference had hit Isabella like a thunderbolt. She had other matrimonial plans for her son. She was totally unwilling that he should become serious about any girl save the one she had chosen for *him*. Certainly she did not wish him to marry *une Anglaise*.

As she had written to her friend the Duc, in the French language which they all used in the palace, and on the greater part of the Island:

"Of course, mon cher, I confide in you as I do in nobody else, and I am troubled though trust I may be putting a more serious construction on the affair which I have described, than is necessary. The good Henri is perhaps too nervous. Dominic is still a boy sowing his wild oats and I do not think I have much cause to be worried about a daughter of an English Foreign Office official. Yet Henri said when he danced with her, he looked at her as though he was infatuated. Then he went out to stolen meetings alone with her. Henri was watching, although my poor son fondly imagined himself quit of both his detective and his secretary. I call him 'poor' because I fear at times he is not as sensible or

wholly absorbed in our island affairs as his father was before him. His interests are too wide-flung. So far he has avoided any discussion on marriage, yet I have warned him that the people are restless. They want him to take a wife and to produce an heir and future Ruler—to ensure that the Principality is safe. We know, you and I, cher ami, that the best thing that could happen is a marriage between my son and your lovely daughter. This would set a seal on the lifelong friendship between Montracine and your ducal line. And the very fact that your daughter Sophie, like Dominic, has Italian blood in her, makes this possible alliance even more agreeable to me.

I intend to give a State Ball on the 30th May which as you know is Dominic's birthday, and I shall do my utmost to persuade him to announce his engagement to darling Sophie that very same day . . ."

A gentle knock on the door—two short taps—informed Isabella that Dominic, himself, had come to bid her good-morning before he started to attend to his affairs of State. It was his habit to knock like that and she called out at once in the most velvet of voices:

"*Ah, c'est toi! entre*—come in, come in, my son."

As Dominic walked into the room, Isabella moved with her serpentine grace to the bureau and slipped the unfinished letter to the Duc inside her blotter.

Dominic came up to her and kissed the long white hand she extended to him—that hand which was so familiar to him, with her favourite ring on the index finger—a magnificent emerald set in diamonds. The one ring among the Crown Jewels which, she had often told Dominic, she would part with only to present to his future wife.

Until now Dominic had never even thought about the ring or to whom it should belong. But this morning he was fascinated by the green beauty of the ring; reminded of those green, glorious eyes which he had likened to emeralds when he had first seen them.

The eyes of Catherine Leigh-Holmes.

"A wonderful morning, mother," he said lightly, and moved on to the veranda. "Let us talk while I enjoy one cigarette before I start work."

"Of course, *chéri*," she said.

They usually conversed in French. The Princesse had always known and deplored the fact that once Dominic grew up he seldom if ever spoke in Italian, although he knew it perfectly. He was an excellent linguist.

She followed him on to the veranda and they sat together under the awning.

It was peaceful and beautiful here, thought Dominic. The Island had never looked lovelier. The vineyards were luxuriant. The silvery olive fields full of promise.

Below the terraces, a beautifully carved stone fountain with three Greek nymphs, their arms entwined, perpetually sprayed crystal water, glittering in the sun. It had been brought here from Athens by Dominic's grandfather, many years ago.

Later, when Isabella herself first came to the Island as a bride, Dominic's father had also made the Italian garden to please her. This, too, was beautiful but the intricate pattern of clipped hedges and the many statues were a little too formal for Dominic's taste. Soon after his Accession, he had installed the fine heated swimming-pool at the back of the palace with a surrounding patio, and barbecue, to suit the more modern among his young relatives and friends.

He had everything, he thought; all that the average young men of his age would enjoy; his racing car, his stable of polo-ponies, his shooting lodge in the mountains, his great wealth. Everything but freedom. The tax on that was brought to mind significantly when he felt his mother's light yet strangely possessive touch on his shoulder.

"My son – shall I ring for more coffee for you?"

He turned to her with his usual sweet smile.

"I have just had breakfast, thank you, Maman."

"I have missed you," she said softly. "Le Petit Palais is not the same without its master."

"I am sure you filled my place admirably while I was away."

"Oh, I am getting old," she said and waited for the expected reply.

"You will never grow old, Maman. Your beauty and your brains make you ageless."

"Always my gallant Dominic," she smiled and sat down gracefully on the chaise-longue opposite him. "Tell me more about your stay in London."

"Thérèse de Palvarias is very crippled these days, poor thing. Of course she sent you her respectful wishes."

"Oh, that silly old woman, I do not want to hear about her."

"She was very kind, and held a splendid reception and dance for me at Claridge's."

"Who did you meet there? Who did you choose for the first dance? Were there some beautiful English *demoiselles*?"

He laughed and answered lightly, although his mind and heart were bright with the memory of Catherine Leigh-Holmes.

"I met many delightful *demoiselles*. Lord Birningham's daughter in particular – Louise – a gorgeous blonde creature."

"I have heard she is nothing more than a mannequin. I find that unattractive for a well-born girl."

Dominic laughed.

"You must not live too much in the past, Maman. Things

are not as they used to be in your girlhood. The Princess of Monaco was once a Hollywood actress. Poor Soraya, a former Queen, is now filming. And I can quote you a dozen and one other names of ex-Crowned Heads engaged in commercial enterprise."

"They do not interest me," said Isabella impatiently. "What other girls did you meet?"

He mentioned many names – all but the one Isabella was angling for. Not once did she hear about the Leigh-Holmes. This very fact roused her keenest anxiety. Could it be that Henri was right when he had said that Dominic had been more than ordinarily interested in the English diplomat's daughter? When subtlety failed, the Princesse resorted to frank attack. She just *had to know*. She persisted:

"Did you by any chance meet that nice Monsieur Leigh-Holmes who came out here when we held our last European Conference?"

She was rewarded by seeing a very slight colour creep up under the tan of her son's handsome face. Rewarded *and* troubled, for he turned that face away as he answered:

"Yes, and I – meant to tell you this last night, but it slipped my mind. I would like you to entertain them. Mr. Leigh-Holmes's daughter, Catherine, is a very clever girl. She graduated last summer from Oxford, then went to Paris. She speaks our language perfectly. You may remember her charming mother who died in an air accident soon after she visited Montracine."

Isabella linked her fingers together and looked down at them.

"I remember, vaguely," she said.

"Catherine – Miss Leigh-Holmes – has heard a great deal about our island from both her parents and she would like to visit us. I want you to write for me if you will and invite Mr. Leigh-Holmes and his daughter to stay with us."

Silence. Isabella half-closed her eyes. Her worst fears were now realised. Leveuve had not exaggerated. But when she spoke to her son it was with the usual touch of honey in her voice.

"But of course, my dear – whatever you wish. Tell me more about Mr. Leigh-Holmes."

"You remember him, Maman," said Dominic impatiently. "It was not so long ago that he stayed in Montracine. He lunched and dined with us just before Sir Mark Daltry took over."

Isabella remembered but was not going to admit it. She did not wish Dominic to think that she had been at all impressed by the English diplomat, although at the time she had admitted that he was the finest type of distinguished intelligent English gentleman.

But it was Catherine she wanted to hear about and for this information that she angled. Now Dominic was forced into being more expansive about Catherine than he had intended.

Yes, she was beautiful. Yes – tall, slim, graceful. Her eyes were exceptional, quite green. She had a clever mind and a modern outlook yet was not too much modernist, etc. etc.

"And did you see much of this paragon?" his mother asked with a bright smile that concealed her annoyance.

She had never known Dominic to speak so flatteringly about any girl.

He parried her questions and was not to be drawn into telling her about any secret meetings with Catherine but when his mother recalled what the secretary had told her, she felt suddenly so angry with Dominic that she could have slapped him. Instead of which she assured him that she would issue an invitation to the Leigh-Holmes whenever he wanted her to. Now she thought he looked positively eager.

"The perfect month on Montracine is May. Let us ask them here for the last week of May."

Now Isabella rose and gripped the balcony railings. Her face was mask-like.

"Ah, but darling, you forget that we shall be very occupied then. Do you not remember the usual celebrations for your birthday? The Island will be *en fête*, and there is the ball taking place in the evening. Le Petit Palais will be full. You know we have already asked many of our relations, and our friends from the mainland, and —"

He interrupted:

"But Maman, this is just what I want – to entertain the Leigh-Holmes royally. They went to a great deal of trouble to be hospitable to me. Catherine will never have a better opportunity of seeing Montracine at its loveliest, and she will enjoy the ball, the music, the gaiety, the native dancing and so on. As for the palace being full, there are plenty of guest-rooms. They will not all be occupied."

Isabella's cheeks reddened with anger. She loathed being frustrated. She had other plans for Dominic – and in particular that one about which she had just written to the Duc d'Arlennes. But she dared not thwart Dominic any further. She knew him too well. He was affectionate and dutiful but he had something of her nature in him, just that something which made him refuse to become a cat's paw in anybody's hands. That, plus the streak of stubbornness which he had inherited from his father. If he wanted the wretched English girl and her father here for the May Celebration then she would not be able to argue him out of it.

By the time he left her, Isabella was in a fine secret temper and the name *Catherine* was already abhorrent to her.

But one thing she was determined to do and that was between now and 30th May, to ensure that Sophie d'Arlennes came often to *Le Petit Palais*, and saw plenty of Dominic.

Beautiful though the English girl might be, she could

not, Isabella decided, be more attractive than the young and aristocratic Sophie whose looks and charm had made her one of the most photographed and sought-after girls in Europe.

Isabella marched imperiously to her telephone. She demanded that she should be put through on her private line to the d'Arlennes' villa which was on the other side of the Island.

She was going to waste no time. She would arrange for Sophie and her father to come up here this very night for an informal dinner party. Just a little private 'welcome home' dinner for dearest Dominic.

During the morning – a day of shimmering Mediterranean sunshine – the Prince drove round Montracine from one village to another, accompanied by his secretary and the First Minister of State.

Gervaise de Reynard was a man more to Isabella's liking than to Dominic's, but perforce he acknowledged de Reynard's judgment in State affairs, his financial genius, and the fact that since Dominic came to power, he had carried out all Dominic's personal wishes. Thousands of the bigger farms and holdings of former landlords here, both French and Italian, who used to conduct their affairs in an avaricious, autocratic manner – long outdated – had been bought by the Crown and divided among the poorer people.

There had been electric changes throughout the Island which had brought a great deal more contentment, and Dominic was contemplating further plans by which the little farmers who had previously been of the peasant-class, would benefit; a matter of investment and company shares. Dominic was, in fact, hoping to run this Island of his not only as a Principality but as a major industry.

He was not sure de Reynard approved of many of these

moves, and there were, on occasions, clashes between the two men in which the Minister was forced to acquiesce.

This morning it certainly seemed to Gervaise de Reynard that his Prince was rapidly gaining in stature and self-confidence. It would not be to de Reynard's benefit if this went too far. He had been so accustomed, in the lifetime of the Prince's father, to holding the reins of power – with the approval of Her Serene Highness, whose personal wealth had been cunningly advanced in many ways by the man whose name so aptly suited him; Reynard . . . *the Fox.*

The sooner the Prince married a suitable girl and provided an heir, and busied himself with a domestic life as well as ruling Montracine, the better.

Otherwise, I shall find myself exiled and living in Monte Carlo with others who have lost their jobs and their fortunes, de Reynard thought savagely.

Wherever they went that golden morning, either on the French or Italian side of the Island, the young Prince was received with a warmth and respect that he found heartening. He spoke to as many people as possible. Never while he was on his Island did he allow an accompanying detective. He feared nothing from his own people. He had a warm word for one and all as he walked among the crowds who rushed to touch him or push their children forward to greet him with little bunches of flowers, and his handsome face glowed. He flung off the boredom and weariness of State affairs. He went back to Le Petit Palais with the welcoming cries of "*Vive le Prince*" still ringing in his ears.

Later that night, after the informal supper party with Sophie and her father was over and the guests had left, Isabella decided to speak firmly to Dominic. To please him, she had invited the Leigh-Holmes for the May Fête and now she was determined to press her advantage.

"I want you to think very seriously about getting married, Dominic."

"Do we have to start this tonight?" he asked impatiently. "It is an old argument. I have told you so many times that I will marry only if and when I fall in love. I refuse to belong to a past when kings and princes were forced to marry the bride chosen for them rather than the one they loved."

"When I looked at Sophie d'Arlennes tonight, I asked myself whether she is not a young girl whom any man would adore?" said Isabella.

Of course, he thought, *this is what Maman wants. This is what I ought to want, too, I suppose, but . . .*

"Sophie is charming but I am not in love with her," he said aloud.

Isabella's eyes suddenly flashed.

"Dominic, my son, you may not realise this but our people are anxious that you should marry. You have waited long enough. The world is full of unrest and just because our Principality happens to be one hundred miles from the mainland and is in many ways less advanced than some, this will not exclude us from the eruptions and dissatisfactions which are taking place in the other world. You are the idol of your people today, but tomorrow . . ." she shrugged her shoulders significantly.

"I know all this," he said, speaking impatiently again. "But I see no signs of dissatisfaction. Everywhere I went this morning, I was given ample proof that I have some sort of popularity."

"You are enormously popular my son, but there are things you do not hear. Nobody would broach the delicate subject of your marriage to you. But your ministers, your advisers, great landholders like our friend d'Arlennes, all are convinced that your marriage now would have a salutary and settling effect on the people."

Dominic looked not at his mother, but at the ground. He was well aware that she was trying to push him into the arms of the charming Sophie. But his heart was a thousand miles away. However, he had no intention of surprising or alarming his mother by so much as hinting that he was so strongly attracted by Edward Leigh-Holmes's daughter. So he said nothing.

The Princesse looked at him uneasily.

"You will recall, Dominic, the great pleasure in Monaco when a son and heir was born to Prince Rainier. Even more so, the dire necessity for an heir that drove the Shah of Persia to get rid of a wife he loved, and to marry another."

Now Dominic gave one of his amused boyish smiles – a smile which even his scheming mother realised with some chagrin was not so often to be seen these days on that brown handsome face. While her husband reigned, Dominic had been such a gay young man. At times Isabella felt he was now weighed down by the difficulties and limitations of his position. But she was ruthlessly ambitious and had no intention of letting him off the leash.

Then he said:

"You know, dear Maman, what the Shah of Persia chose to do was his own affair. I admit that as a ruling Prince it would be a good idea for me to marry and have an heir. But this must wait until I make my decision."

That left Isabella feeling frustrated and still more uneasy because she had no real idea whether that decision concerned Sophie or not. However, she was too subtle a woman to persist in any argument that might make him feel the iron hand and draw away from her. She kissed him good-night with affection and went to her suite.

But Dominic did not go to his own rooms. He stepped out on to the terrace and hands in his pockets, stared up at the sky which was ablaze with crystalline stars. The Island looked magical and mysterious in this light. A jewel set in the Mediterranean, he thought, and half-ashamedly felt an extraordinary desire to go to his desk and write a poem. A poem to *her*. Instead of which he found an English volume of verses and turned to Byron. He read aloud:

> "*She walks in beauty, like the night*
> *Of cloudless climes and starry skies;*
> *And all that's best of dark and bright*
> *Meet in her aspect and her eyes.*"

He closed the book again and felt a bit of a fool. In this day and age poets were considered fools, he supposed. It would be better perhaps if he could prefer electronics to English verse.

But it described *her* – from the moment he had seen her. For him, the Prince of Montracine, Catherine had 'walked in beauty like the night' – a glorious Mediterranean night of stars and moon and ineffable peace – such as this. 'Her eyes are *green* and bright,' he thought, then he said aloud:

"I will not marry Sophie d'Arlennes," and it was as well that Isabella in her own rooms at the far end of Le Petit Palais, could not hear those words.

7

The silver-blue Rolls flying the white and gold flag of Montracine was the first thing that Catherine saw as the private plane piloted by the Captain of the Prince's own Flight, touched down on the Island airstrip. Then she had eyes only for the young man who stepped out of the Rolls and walked towards her.

His Serene Highness, Prince Dominic of Montracine, in person. Catherine was really rather annoyed with herself because her body began suddenly to burn. A deep joy pervaded her whole being.

This was wonderful! He had kept his word. It had not been just an idle invitation issued when they had first met in London. She and her father had received a personal letter from the Princesse asking them here for the celebrations which she wrote, always took place on the 30th May to commemorate her son's birthday.

"I say!" Edward Leigh-Holmes had exclaimed with a broad smile when he had handed this letter to his daughter when it came. "Big stuff! This will be no ordinary holiday and of course, I don't know whether it's your charms or mine which have worked the trick."

"Yours, of course, Daddy," Catherine had answered gaily.

But feeling almost guilty, she was aware that the Prince had wanted *her* to go to Montracine. She had received a telephone call from him which told her that the invitation from his mother was on its way, and expressed the hope that her father would apply for this week's leave in good time and be in a position to accept.

"Royal command," Edward Leigh-Holmes had said with his tongue in his cheek, "I dare say I can fix it. I'll drop a line to Sir Mark and tell him what's afoot – if he doesn't already know."

Sir Mark Daltry wrote back that he did know and that it was a splendid time to visit the Island because tremendous preparations were already in hand for the May celebrations.

Right from the start it had been a thrilling flight for Catherine. V.I.P. reception at Heathrow, luxurious seats in the beautiful private aircraft. Two Montracineans who were returning to the Island and to whom the Prince was giving a lift, travelled with them. Otherwise the Leigh-Holmes had the royal plane to themselves.

They left England in mist and low-lying cloud, but landed on Montracine in brilliant sunshine. As soon as Catherine stepped out of the aircraft she felt the benison of the warm sun and was glad she had packed one or two summery dresses. After all that she had heard about the Island it was exciting to look down as they circled lower, and she could see Montracine from a thousand feet up. It looked interesting – dotted with forests, criss-crossed with rivers and roads, and red-roofed buildings. As she said to her father: "*Quite a place!*"

Apart from her personal admiration for Dominic – and she had to admit that she had thought of him far too often – it was a thrill to be on the Island, at last, and to know that she was to be a guest at Le Petit Palais. During the flight she had half-wondered if she had been building up too glowing a picture of the young Prince, but the moment she saw him again she knew otherwise. He was all that she had imagined. His large dark eyes brimmed with enthusiasm and a warmth of welcome which he had made no effort to hide.

"Welcome to Montracine," he said to them both, and when Catherine would have curtsied, quickly prevented her. "Please – *no* – this is not an official visit. I want no ceremony."

He brushed the back of her hand with his lips but not before his gaze met and held hers fully. She found herself growing as embarrassed and tongue-tied as a schoolgirl and hoped madly that he would like the outfit she had chosen for the flight – bought, of course, for such a special occasion. She had spent all and more than this year's allowance on clothes, and remembering her University days of slacks and jerseys and that old camel hair coat, she wondered if she were the same Catherine. Daddy had told her that she looked very smart. A striped blue and white silk dress, and jacket, with sailor collar, white-braided. A Homburg-shaped white straw hat with blue binding at a jaunty angle on her chestnut head. Over her arms she carried a short white coat with gilt buttons.

The Prince had come to meet them in informal dress; dark blue slacks, a blue sports jacket and white shirt. He looked very young – so like any ordinary well-dressed young man with no pretensions – no throne she thought. He was never pompous. She *did* like him. And she was childishly pleased because she had chosen her own navy and white outfit. It seemed almost a complement of his.

When they were in the Rolls being driven away from the airstrip and through the town, Dominic talked in his courteous way to Edward Leigh-Holmes but his gaze turned frequently to the young girl as he pointed out anything that he thought would be of interest to her.

Already Catherine was fascinated by the sight of the Montracine policemen in their smart white shorts, white linen coats, and the funny little three-cornered hats – black, shiny, with a large M in gold at the front. She was to grow used to seeing that M everywhere: Montracine. The Island was like something out of a story book, yet the gay little Port seemed busy; the harbour was full of handsome boats. There were some excellent looking shops in the town centre and crowds of people. Girls with mini-skirts or flowered summer dresses. Young men in casual sports clothes. The tree-lined boulevards were crowded and the cafés with their small tables under the awning all out of doors, looked busy – gay and inviting.

The avenue of plane trees, which was the main thoroughfare, was shady and fresh with the light green leaves of the early summer. There were flower-beds everywhere – for the most part filled with scarlet carnations.

"*We-ll!*" said Catherine starry-eyed, as she looked out of the window, "I'm glad I brought my new camera."

Dominic smiled and pointed to an ornate gabled building with the Montracine flag flying from an upper window.

"Our Palais de Justice. Those iron gateways lead into the Law Courts and the *avocats* chambers. Now – you see that new-looking white building – that is our Town Library where, of course, we have many English books."

"Currency troubles or not, I shall enjoy shopping tomorrow," she laughed.

"Perhaps not tomorrow," he said, "because a great many of our big shops will be closed. They are putting up the decorations for Saturday. Flags across the streets and so on. Then there is a Fair coming over from the mainland. One of these open-air shows that you see sometimes in the streets along the French coast. It may amuse you."

Everything amused Catherine. In particular, she enjoyed the beauty of the countryside. The serene graceful palms – the cork trees, the terraced vineyards, the olive-groves and the prosperous-looking apple orchards. The small white-washed farms were enchanting she thought, and now and again they passed an imposing château owned by a well-to-do Montracinean and visible at the far end of a long tree-fringed drive.

At last, after climbing a long steep hill, Catherine, for the first time, saw a royal residence – Le Petit Palais. Perched high up, the frontage of the fine white building was serpentine in design, with tall rounded windows and one beautiful turret from which a flag rippled in the breeze. A flag which showed that the reigning Prince was home. The grace and dignity of the white classic pillars supporting the loggias brought an exclamation of pleasure from Catherine.

"Oh, how lovely!"

"I am glad you think so," said Dominic. "Your father of course knows Le Petit Palais quite well."

"Know and admire it," said Mr. Leigh-Holmes. "It has none of the rococo ornamentation that spoil so many royal buildings. It is one of the most beautiful little palaces in the world."

"Thank you," said Dominic, obviously pleased.

Catherine sat speechless, drinking in the sight of the glorious architecture – so simple, so dignified, so serene. Most of the windows were shielded from the Mediterranean sun by blue and white sun-blinds, with white fringe. She had never seen anything more glamorous than the brilliant pink and scarlet of the bouganvillaea massed against those white walls, some reaching as high as the wrought-iron balconies of the upper windows.

The two polished entrance doors were open. Now for the first time, Catherine noted the livery of the royal staff. Two young men in dark blue suits with gold buttons and epaulettes came running down to open the car doors and help with the luggage.

"My mother's private suite and my rooms are on the other side of the palace," Dominic informed Catherine. "We look across our English and Italian gardens, and down to the sea. I have instructions from my mother to take you straight to her, so that she can welcome you."

For a moment, as Catherine and her father followed the Prince up the wide marble steps, she felt a sudden doubt as to whether she really liked all this magnificence, or whether in her heart she was not the sort of girl who preferred a casual atmosphere and complete lack of formality. Whatever Dominic said about this being an unofficial visit it was not going to be casual or relaxing. She would have to be at her 'best' all the time, and she was just about to meet one of the most powerful and famous women in Europe. It was a little nerve-racking, to say the least of it. On the other hand Dominic had given them such a warm and friendly welcome and the whole set-up was so thrilling, Catherine could not help enjoying it. She received only a brief impression of the spacious hall which stretched to the windows on the other side of the building, of tapestry-covered walls, a dark-green marble floor, long marble tables on curved gilded legs, bearing silver-gilt candelabra, fine porcelain figurines, jewelled boxes, huge displays of flowers in tall vases, and magnificent flowering plants.

A beautiful double staircase of wrought-iron and polished wood, the wide stairs thickly carpeted, led up to a minstrel's gallery, hung with fine Gobelin tapestries and paintings.

This, Catherine thought, with growing excitement, was a palace indeed. Le Petit Palais – rightly named because splendid and imposing though it was, it had none of the chilling (what Catherine privately termed 'putting off') sensation that one often got in huge buildings. It had begun to seem as welcoming to her as it was beautiful. And it was Dominic's ancestral home.

The hall seemed full of people hurrying to and fro, bent on their various missions—mostly staff, she supposed, as they bowed politely to their Prince, standing by to let him pass. For each one he had a quick word, a bright and friendly smile.

The lean remembered figure of Henri Leveuve now appeared. He stopped to add his word of welcome to the Leigh-Holmes. Catherine caught a direct glance from his cold eye and found it as antagonistic and unattractive as it had seemed in London.

Besides, Leveuve was a fat double-chinned man in an immaculate white suit, and with horn-rimmed glasses. He could not have been more effusive or complimentary when Dominic introduced the guests to him.

This then was Monsieur de Reynard, Dominic's First Minister of State. The Reynard—a 'fat fox', she thought, with some amusement. Was he as affable as he appeared? Or did he gobble up any little chickens that got in his way? She had always had a respect for her own intuition. She was rarely wrong about people. Intuitively she did not take to the bowing, smiling, hearty Monsieur de Reynard. He was so enchanted to see his dear friend, Mr. Leigh-Holmes again, he said. Remembered so well his last visit to Montracine. It was an honour that this time his so beautiful daughter should be with him. Etc. etc. All of which Catherine took with a grain of salt.

Dominic cut short the Minister's effusions.

Her Serene Highness awaited them, and they were already late, he said.

As they walked up one of the lovely staircases, Dominic spoke to Catherine:

"We will not stop now but before you go, I will, if I may, bring you back here and show you the Palace collection of paintings. You are interested in the fine arts, are you not?"

"I am, indeed," she said.

At the end of a long marble-floored corridor, two liveried footmen opened tall double doors. Catherine now felt that she was entering another world. This was the private wing, sacrosanct to Dominic's famous mother.

For an inexplicable reason, some of Catherine's excitement and enthusiasm suddenly waned. It was as though a chill hand had touched her. She almost said:

'*No – no – don't go on. I want to turn back. I do not want . . .*'

What didn't she want? She did not know and had no time to think. But her nerves were suddenly stabilised by the calm familiar voice of her father.

"I told you, didn't I, Catherine, that this was the loveliest royal home in Europe."

"You are very kind," said Dominic with his charming smile.

Catherine now found herself in a salon of great elegance and distinction. Dominic told her that it was here his mother entertained her personal friends. Not too large, although the ceiling was high and painted exquisitely green, gold and rose – with charming clusters of cupids and nymphs, in true Italian style. Her Serene Highness obviously favoured the décor of her own country.

Three tall windows opened on to a canopied balcony. They were framed in gold brocaded Florentine curtains. Above the high mantelpiece hung a glorious Venetian mirror. The low luxurious chairs and sofa were of ivory-studded satin heaped with little velvet and gold embroidered cushions.

On a snow-leopard rug lay a beautiful wolfhound who, as the visitors entered, got up on to his paws and growled very softly – a growl that turned to a note of welcome as he ran towards Dominic who laid a hand on the animal's head.

"This is Sulla, my mother's great pet."

"There you are, Catherine," said Mr. Leigh-Holmes with a smile. "You've always said that this is the sort of dog you would like to keep if we didn't live in London."

Catherine held out a hand and tried to coax Sulla towards her, but the dog backed away, growling again. She could see they were not going to be friends.

A woman's voice interrupted them – a low-pitched slightly imperious voice speaking perfect English.

Catherine turned and saw that Her Serene Highness, Princesse Isabella, had joined them.

For a split second Catherine once more experienced a curious sense of cold, and discomfort, as she looked into the dark brilliant eyes of Dominic's mother. The woman who appeared to dominate Montracine.

She might have known that it was his mother, Catherine reflected. They had the same colouring and fine tall figures. But Dominic's eyes were so much larger and softer and his generous mouth had nothing in common with the thin-cut lips of the Princesse.

It was a tense moment for Catherine. Not every day did a girl like herself come as a guest to the home of a woman of Isabella's world-wide reputation. Catherine decided that she felt scared but the frightened feeling vanished as she started to curtsy to Her Serene Highness, for with much charm, Isabella prevented her from doing so and held out a friendly hand.

"I am so delighted to meet you at last, Miss Leigh-Holmes, and to see your admirable father again. We all remember his former visit to Montracine with pleasure."

Catherine, scarlet-cheeked, murmured her thanks. Afterwards when she had time to think about it all, she remembered the extraordinary dryness of the cold fingers that clasped hers for that fleeting moment. Cold, even on a day like this which to Catherine seemed positively baking.

Isabella was certainly handsome, and she made Catherine feel small and insignificant. The Princesse had great dignity – and, as might be expected – was perfectly dressed in black tailored linen, with touches of white at the throat and one fabulous emerald and diamond brooch pinned to her shoulder. The hand she had held out to Catherine was also bejewelled and sparkled. But she was graciousness itself. She took them all out on to her terrace where there were marble-topped tables and comfortable basket chairs, and told them that drinks would be served to them. They must be thirsty. It was a hot morning, in another hour they would lunch and as the weather was so perfect, she said, the meal was being served in her private garden under the lime-trees.

It was soon made plain to Catherine that while Her Serene Highness was in the room no one else had much chance of speaking. The Princesse dominated the conversation.

And she tries to dominate her son, just as Daddy said, thought Catherine.

The girl, herself, had never felt less bright or communicative. *She* was being 'dominated', she thought with wry amusement. Mesmerised! Like a foolish schoolgirl, all she seemed able to do was to say '*Yes, Madame*', or '*No, Madame*', and when finally the Princesse engaged Mr. Leigh-Holmes in conversation, and Dominic moved his chair a fraction closer to Catherine's and began to talk to her, she still felt awkward.

But now and again, when her gaze met his, all of life seemed to stand still for her. There was such undisguised interest and admiration in his eyes.

He murmured to her in a voice so low that his mother could not hear:

"Do not look scared. My august Maman is not really so frightening and I promise you your visit here will not be too formal. I want so much to show you my Island without a hint of protocol."

"I would like that," she said and her heart beat a little faster.

She relaxed then and sipped her long iced '*orange pressé*'. She marvelled at the view across the magnificent Italian garden. Those hedges, she thought, the dark green of the sculptured peacocks, the perfect planning was a miracle of topiary. Still more did she appreciate the view of the distant mountains, amethyst-coloured, the beautifully laid-out farms, the silvery olives, the young green corn, terrace upon terrace of vineyards, little churches with quaint bell-towers, white cottages with green or red tiled roofs. It was a bright, miniature country – with every sign of peace and plenty – which seemed sweet and remote from the power struggle going on in the rest of the world. Yet when she looked at and listened to the Prince's mother, Catherine could well imagine the struggle for power took place here, too, on this miraculous Island.

Down in the busy port, life was modern and active. But behind it all an interesting little battle between past, present and future was going on. Catherine's quick mind fastened on this fact. Yet when she looked into the eyes of the young man who was at the head of a unique Principality, all such thought slipped away, leaving her to dwell only on the quiet radiance of the sun on the blue water, stretching between Montracine and the coast of France. She listened dreamily to the chime of church bells, and smelled the delicate fragrance of some creamy flowering vine unknown to her, climbing up to the balcony.

She was reduced to uneasiness again only when Isabella involved her in a discussion about herself. The Princesse wanted to know exactly what she did in England (or had done). This time Catherine spoke in French because

Dominic's mother addressed her in that language. It was a challenge to Catherine. If her French was to be criticised she had confidence that she could speak it as well if not better than most English girls.

A little reluctantly, perhaps, Isabella complimented her.

"Your accent is very good," she said graciously. "Do you also speak my mother tongue?" And she made a remark, rapidly, in Italian.

Catherine felt rather than saw that Dominic was watching and listening. She thanked her lucky stars that she had also taken Italian in order to get her degree. So the Princesse's narrow brows went up and she nodded as Catherine answered in excellent Italian.

"Very good."

"Languages were Miss Leigh-Holmes's subject, Maman," put in Dominic. "We have a young Bachelor of Arts with us, you know."

"Very good," repeated the Princesse and added with a sweet yet freezing smile: "I find it hard to understand why all these girls today seem to think of little but—what is it called? The 'O' Levels—'A' Levels—Bachelor of Arts—all such things. *Tiens!* Women will soon cease to be truly feminine. I find it sad."

Catherine said nothing but Dominic laughed.

"My dear Maman, I know of no one more truly feminine than our guest and I think she would like you to call her Catherine. Miss Leigh-Holmes is so very formal."

Isabella put her tongue in her cheek but smiled.

"This being your time of fiesta, my son, let us by all means waive formality."

That was what she *said*, but Catherine was quite sure it was not what she wanted. And the Princesse continued to call her Miss Leigh-Holmes.

Lunch was certainly a formal affair, but in a perfect

setting under a canopy of green vines on the terrace. Seated at a beautiful round marble table, they were served by young Montracinean waiters now dressed in white and with white gloves on their hands. A delicious meal of young veal, preceded by the langoustines caught locally. Wine, white or red, was poured into exquisite Venetian goblets.

Time certainly rolled back here, thought Catherine. Whatever was happening elsewhere, Isabella did not intend to dispense with class distinction and gracious living at Le Petit Palais. And it was on such subjects, so Catherine discovered, that she clashed continually with her son.

Catherine made no comments to her father. She knew that as a trained diplomat he was more used to a punctilious ceremonial atmosphere than herself, and much less sensitive to the personality of Her Serene Highness who within these first few hours of arrival, Catherine learned to fear. She was handsome – cultured – essentially regal – and she was Dominic's mother. But Catherine would never like her. She stood for everything that the girl most disliked.

She was supposed to go to her room and rest after lunch. The *siesta* was part and parcel of the Montracinean life. It was very warm between two and four.

But Catherine felt too restless to lie down. At first she explored her luxurious bedroom. Such a grand room, with long French windows. They were shuttered now against the hot Mediterranean sun. It was a room designed for a luxury-loving woman. The décor was all in white with delicate French painted furniture and a wide low bed draped with ivory quilted satin, embroidered at the four corners with green water lilies. The ceiling itself was a delight, painted in palest blue with the same motif of lilies. The curtains were a deep amethyst gauze ornamented with silver thread. Everywhere Catherine looked she found beauty: handsome ornaments, fine Venetian mirrors, velvet-framed paintings, books and magazines. The bathroom itself a miracle of pale green marble with silver fittings.

Catherine had been told by Isabella that one of her own maids had been detailed to look after her. She had only to ring. Everything had been unpacked when Catherine came up from lunch. It had somewhat embarrassed her. The Montracinean girl must have found such humble luggage as Catherine possessed, very dull. Catherine wondered if the girl had ever even heard of Marks & Spencers, where Catherine bought most of her lingerie and cotton frocks.

Goodness, she thought, *it's going to be difficult not to put a foot wrong in this place. Her Serene Highness is a bit of a tyrant and I reckon she does not really want me here. Is she afraid that her son—?*

But Catherine cut short her own reflections. What in heaven's name had Her Highness to be *afraid* of? Suddenly Catherine felt quite weak as she remembered the last words Dominic had said to her as they finished lunch:

"I am so very happy to have you here, Catherine."

That was not 'protocol'. That was genuine and heart-warming, like the long warm look from his marvellous eyes.

She couldn't rest. She felt too vigorous – too excited.

She changed from her suit into a short blue cotton frock, and bare-legged, with her feet in straw sandals, found her way out of Le Petit Palais and into the grounds.

8

Careless of the sun on her bare head, or the fact that she was probably doing the wrong thing by coming out alone like this, Catherine began to explore the royal grounds. Having found her way to the English rose garden, she continued as far as a small ornamental lake on the banks of which a miniature Greek temple in white marble had been built. It was obviously used as a summer-house – a sort of 'Folly'. She carried on, through a cedar-grove, cool and dark, then came out into the sunshine again. Now she found herself at the back of the palace. Here, a more modern world existed. With delight she saw the magnificent swimming-pool, kidney-shaped, blue as the sea and with a sheltered terrace and barbecue at one end. Only one person was in sight – Dominic himself. He was wearing nothing but a pair of blue trunks, and he was lying on a white rubber mattress in the sun.

With frank admiration Catherine looked down at that perfectly proportioned muscular young body with the long slim legs and wide shoulders. How brown he was! His eyes were hidden behind dark glasses. His hands were laced behind his head. He might, she thought, be asleep.

She turned to walk away but Dominic must have sensed that somebody was watching him. He took off his glasses and sat up. As he saw the young girl in her short blue dress, he called to her eagerly:

"Ah! Catherine! So you have found your way here! But how delightful. I thought you would be indoors sleeping."

She moved towards him, happy and at ease with him again.

"I'm not one to do much resting. How gorgeous the pool looks. Have you been in?"

"Several times."

"It looks tempting."

"Why not come in and swim with me?"

"Oh, ought I to – ?" she began.

"You ought to do anything you wish to do," he broke in. "Do you like swimming?"

"I adore it."

"Then please, Catherine, if you have brought your things – go and change."

"Maybe it won't be right – I mean I've only got a bikini. Perhaps it isn't done here – I mean – oh, what an idiot I am – but sometimes on the Continent they like you to wear a *proper* suit!"

He roared with laughter.

"My dear sweet Catherine, it doesn't matter here at all. You will not be the first girl to wear a bikini on the Island. It is permitted, I assure you."

All the same, I wonder if his mother would approve, Catherine found herself thinking.

But her thoughts carried her no further. This was a temptation she did not want to resist.

In no time she had run back to Le Petit Palais and up to her suite. When she rejoined the Prince she was wearing her white bikini suit, and a short towelling robe. She carried a frilled white swim-cap in one hand, and her dark glasses in the other.

"I've brought my sunburn cream, too," she told Dominic. "I'm sure it's necessary."

"For you, yes. You need to get used to our sun. It can scorch."

She sat down beside him, folded her arms around her hunched knees and drew a long breath.

"Oh, this is gorgeous. I can't believe that only a few hours ago I was in London."

"And I can hardly believe that you are here," he said in a low voice. "We have been friends such a short time, Catherine, yet I feel that I have known you for centuries."

She had no answer for that, but her heart beat fast. She murmured:

"I forgot my cigarettes."

"Do you need to smoke so much?"

"I don't really smoke much – it's more nerves than anything," she said, laughing.

"But do you have such bad nerves, Catherine?"

"Not really. No – not at all. Actually I smoke less than any of my friends. It's only when I am —"

"When you are what?"

His glasses were off. He was sitting quite close to her and looking at her with an earnest gaze that she found disturbing.

"Oh, when I'm *nervous*," she blurted out.

"You are not nervous with me, surely."

She resorted to laughter.

"Of course I am. It's the first time I've ever gone swimming with – with – a man like you."

"Catherine, please don't speak or behave as though I am different from any other man," he said, and now he spoke quite abruptly. "There's nothing I dislike more than being treated as a person apart."

"Oh, I'm sorry. I'm so tactless," she said, confused.

"No, you are not," he said quickly. "I can understand that you feel a little awkward, but I beg you not to. Just be as relaxed and happy as you were that night with me in London when we ate out together. I am the same person, you know, even within the precincts of my own palace."

"I know you are, Dominic."

"How well do you swim, Catherine?" he asked, suddenly.

"Ordinarily well, and I'm rather a good diver."

Dominic sprang to his feet, held out a hand and pulled her up beside him.

"After that piece of boasting you shall show what you can do, *ma petite*."

She let her robe fall. Now Dominic looked for the fraction of a moment at the slim perfection of the girl in that ivory bikini. The symmetry of her young graceful limbs, the beauty of her skin, so camellia-white after the sun-browned bodies he was used to seeing out here, the loveliness of her unspoiled youth, caught him by the throat. She was like a classic nymph standing there beside the blue pool, he thought. More than a little alluring with the bronze waves of her hair tumbled about her flushed face.

She did not meet his eyes. Pulling on her cap, pushing her long hair into it, she brushed past him and ran to the diving-board – the highest one – and swift and lithe, dived into the glittering water. With sheer pleasure he watched that swallow dive. She was, indeed, like a snow-bird, he thought. When she rose to the surface he looked down into her wet laughing face and felt all the warmth and longing of his own passionate heart.

"Don't stay out there, cheat," she gasped. "Come on in."

So he dived in and they swam together, laughing, talking and completely natural and happy in each other's company. When they came out of the water again and she sat mopping her wet face with her towel, Dominic walked to the barbecue. He returned with cigarettes and a lighter.

"Now you shall feed your nervous system," he laughed.

They sat smoking together while the warm sun drank up every drop of water from their hot young bodies.

"It was wonderful water – not too cold – just perfect," she said.

"And you are a wonderful swimmer, Catherine."

"I told you I was," she giggled.

"You are still such a child."

"You know that I'm not."

"I do not mean altogether. In fact I know you are a very clever young woman but at heart you are still a child."

"I think we are all like that, really, Dominic."

"I wish I were," he said suddenly. "I long to be but I find it difficult in my life – often impossible."

"I understand."

"You understand everything. Catherine, I am not just flattering you idly when I tell you that I am happier with you than I have ever been with anybody in my life."

She coloured and smoked her cigarette more quickly.

"I find it hard to believe."

"All the same it is true. I feel completely at ease with you. In fact I find you adorable."

She was enthralled but deliberately ignored his praise.

"And you happen to be one of the most popular princes in Europe," she said.

"Poor princes," he said with a short laugh, "they are not always to be envied."

"But you do as you want up to a point, don't you, Dominic? You are not as bound and fettered today as ruling princes used to be."

"That is true. Here in my own grounds for instance, we are more or less free from spying eyes, but I assure you that if one photographer broke through the cordon and found his way down here this moment and snapped us, our photographs would be in every paper in the world."

Catherine thought it best to laugh this off.

"I wouldn't mind – would you, Your Serene Highness?"

"If you want to know the truth, Catherine, I would not."

Silence. The languid hot silence of the siesta hour on the enchanted island.

My God, thought Catherine, *this mustn't go on. I can't play the fool with him nor he with me. It won't do.*

She was totally unprepared for his next move. Suddenly he stubbed out his cigarette-end, caught one of her hands and kissed it.

"I find you so adorable," he said for the second time.

Mad happiness gripped her. She could neither move nor speak. The silence between them was broken by the long harsh scream of the white peacocks that roamed Isabella's Italian garden. It was stupid, Catherine thought, but it seemed almost like a warning cry from *her* – from Isabella. Catherine moved away from her royal companion, spread out her towel and threw herself face downward upon it.

"I must try to get brown," she said.

"You will burn. You must be careful, Catherine."

She felt that she was burning already, mentally as well as physically. She felt chaotic. She no longer wanted to lie there beside him in the sun. In a queer sort of way she did not want to be alone with *him* like this. Yet he was the one man in the world she *did* want to be with. She was in a daze.

"Please forgive me," she stuttered, "I – I think I will go in and rest. It's been wonderful – the swimming – everything. Thank you."

At once with his innate courtesy, he stood up and gave that little bow of the head which was familiar now.

"I quite understand. After tea, if your father would like it, I will take you both to La Cina. It is the oldest and most unspoilt village in our Island. There will be a special fiesta there the day after tomorrow. They roast an ox in the market-place and drink their special wine and the boys and girls dress in national costume and dance for me. As a rule they present me with a birthday present – something they have made. The natives of La Cina are famous for their exquisite cedarwood furniture, boxes and ornaments. Ever since I was a child they have given me something which I value. I cannot tell them that I already have one room in the palace overflowing with their kind gifts," Dominic added, and his laughter broke the tension that had been mounting in Catherine.

"It sounds terrific!" she said and he laughed again.

"I do like that very English word of approval, TER-RIFIC. It amuses me. You, too, Catherine, are ter-rific!"

She fingered her swim-cap with damp nervous fingers. How foolish she was to be so disturbed – to feel so exalted – because the Prince of Montracine said things like this to her. She did not know why. She really did not care. She was once more content to let a joyous wave of happiness roll over her.

"Come," Dominic said, taking her arm, "I will walk back with you. I have had enough swimming for the day and I must do some work. I confess that my desk is littered. I must get Leveuve on to some of the overflow. Business – affairs of State, etc. Good-bye for a few hours to freedom – to this ter-rific friendship."

"Not good-bye to friendship, I hope," said Catherine with an amused glance at him.

"Of course not."

He stopped dead. They had just reached the courtyard at the back of the palace. Turning swiftly Catherine saw the figure of the very man Dominic had just mentioned. Henri Leveuve was approaching them.

The private secretary looked no less formidable arrayed for the swimming-pool and in a striped bathrobe, than when he was immaculately dressed, Catherine thought. Somehow that pallid face, always with a blue suspicion of moustache and beard, revolted her. And those protuberant eyes looked at her with what she felt to be a definite antagonism.

Dominic, however, greeted Leveuve with just the right touch of authority, coupled with charm.

"Ah, Leveuve! You and I are out of touch with the timing of this excellent relaxation. I have just finished, and am going in to work. No matter. Join me later."

"Certainly, sir," Leveuve bowed. "Would you prefer that I come at once?"

"No, indeed, *mon ami*, enjoy your swim."

As Dominic and Catherine walked on, the secretary looked over his shoulder and watched the two cross into the shadow of the building and disappear.

He looked towards the swimming-pool, then back again, and flinging his towel over one shoulder, seemed to change his mind and walked back into the palace through the staff entrance.

Once in his own bedroom he lifted the house phone and demanded to be put through to Her Serene Highness. A few moments after that, Isabella, who had been resting in her large cool room dimmed by closed shutters, rose, drew the shutters aside and walked on to her balcony. Now she saw exactly what Dominic's secretary had seen. Her son and the English girl walking close together round the clump of palm trees to the left of the palace, and to the front entrance. With the intelligence that had been passed on to her, she knew exactly where they had been. Catherine had not gone to her room for a siesta. She had been down there in the pool with Dominic. Whether he had invited her to do so, or she had just taken it into her head to pursue him, Isabella did not know. But at the sight of her son's brown laughing face and the girl's equally happy one as she looked up at him, the watching woman's hands clenched. Her lips tightened into a thin line.

She went back into her room and began, angrily, to pace up and down. Her thoughts were far from pleasurable. That wretched girl! It was obvious that Dominic had formed a new and close friendship with the Leigh-Holmes while he was in London. He had forced her, his mother, to invite them here this week, and for no ordinary reason she was sure. Seldom had she seen him look so carefree – so content. She ought to have been pleased – to value her son's personal happiness. But the reverse feeling made her very gorge rise because of Catherine Leigh-Holmes. She was a clever, well-bred girl, better, perhaps, than many of the young English women who came to this Island, and were presented to Her Highness. Certainly she was unusually good-looking, too, and had excellent manners, and many other attributes. But that she should become an intimate friend of Dominic's was not to be tolerated. Under no circumstances must the ruler of this Principality fall in love with an English girl, a *commoner* – and wreck all Isabella's plans for his marriage to Sophie d'Arlennes.

Isabella stopped in front of one of her long mirrors. Clenching and unclenching her fingers, she stared at the reflection of her own bitter face.

"I will not endure a close friendship between my son and that English girl," she muttered the words aloud, "*I will not.*"

But powerful autocrat though she was, used to getting her own way, she did not quite see how she was going to avert this catastrophe – if such a catastrophe was to be. Or were she and Leveuve taking the affair too seriously? After all, there was nothing very significant about two young people choosing to swim together.

But that look on Dominic's face.

Haunted by it, Isabella rang imperiously for her maid and started to dress. She had a strong inclination to send for Catherine and offer to take her out at once and entertain her, just in order to get her away from Dominic. But she was frustrated because she had an important engagement at four o'clock with a certain Baron Wulffheim, an Austrian diplomat, and his wife, who were coming to visit her today. She could not cancel it because the Baroness was an old schoolfriend and had made the long journey from Vienna especially to talk to her. Bitterly, Isabella considered the fact that the Leigh-Holmes had only just arrived and would be here for another few days. It had aggravated her from the start because Dominic had insisted on them coming before the rest of the guests who were to arrive tomorrow. If Dominic was in fact seriously interested in this girl, she, his mother, must step in and nip the affair in the bud. The problem was *how* to achieve it. How? *How?*

It was fortunate for Catherine and Dominic that the Princesse was prevented from going to La Cina and spoiling their day.

9

The visit to La Cina had been fascinating. The people had been so gay and Dominic had been a marvellous host and what Catherine remembered most about the day was the moment when Dominic had turned his head swiftly, almost as though under a strange compulsion and looked straight into her eyes. Catherine found it impossible to forget that long deep look from the Prince. It could mean nothing. It could mean everything. All she knew was that it had in some curious way burnt into her consciousness and left a mark there.

Her father remarked, that night, that she was quiet and rather pale but she laughed this off and told him it was just the sudden heat after the cool May days at home.

Tomorrow, when so many relatives and guests would be arriving at Le Petit Palais there was to be a big dinner party. It would be a tiring day. Catherine and her father dined with Isabella and the Prince quietly. Afterwards they drank coffee in the Princesse's private drawing-room.

Her Serene Highness was voluble, brilliant as usual but Catherine found the young Prince unusually silent. Now and again when she stole a glance at him, aware of her rapid heart-beats, he did not return her gaze and seemed almost to wish to avoid it.

What have I done, she wondered. *Did that look mean in some way that I have offended him?*

But she couldn't think what. Finally she told herself that

she was just being foolish. But she was glad when the Princesse herself suggested an early retirement and they went to their own suites.

Catherine did not immediately undress. She stepped out on to her balcony. The sky was ablaze with stars. The lights from the Port of Montracine twinkled below the hill. All was quiet save for the faint sound of distant music.

It was a night of enchantment and Catherine felt suddenly unwilling to go to bed. Her fatigue had gone.

Quite definitely she had not enjoyed this evening, she decided. Now she would enjoy it, alone. She put a white wool coat over her shoulders, for the Mediterranean night was cool with a little wind blowing from the sea, and made her way downstairs.

The palace was quiet although lights burned in the magnificent Picture Gallery and corridors. One or two servants still moved around, intent on their affairs. One of them, a young footman, opened the double door for Catherine, bowing respectfully as she walked out of the palace.

She sauntered through the Princesse's fine Italian garden, and came eventually to the small white temple with its circular roof and graceful Ionic pillars. Dominic had told her that sometimes in the heat of the summer, he retired there to read his books, for it was cool and peaceful inside.

She stopped in front of the Folly, hands in the pockets of her coat, and looked up at the tall cypress trees on either side. There was a pungent odour of herbs in the air. A night-bird called suddenly, shrilly. The wind capriciously blew Catherine's long hair across her eyes.

"Oh, how beautiful it is here!"

Unconsciously she spoke these words aloud. She was thoroughly startled when a man's voice said:

"And how beautiful *you* are, Mam'selle."

Catherine was not nervous. She was used to dealing with all types, but she had to confess she was a little disquietened by the sight of the figure that suddenly confronted her. A strange tall young man with wild yellow hair, uncombed and tangled and, in her opinion, he had mad blue eyes. The moonlight showed him up distinctly. He wore a pair of shabby jeans and a torn dirty jersey.

She wondered what to say, reflecting ruefully that she really ought not to have come into the grounds alone. But she looked the man squarely in the eyes.

"Good-evening," she said casually. "You spoke in English. Are you not a Montracinean?"

"My father was French. My mother, English. I speak both languages," he said with a strong accent, and grinned at her – rocking she thought, a trifle tipsily, backwards and forwards on his toes.

"Well, if you don't mind I am going back to the palace," she said, and began to walk boldly past him.

He caught her by the arm.

"Not so fast. You're a real beauty. I saw that, the moment I got near you. You're not an islander, either. Are you one of the maids up in Le Petit Palais?"

Catherine pulled her arm away. She was beginning to feel distinctly frightened by this big hulking fellow.

"I'm a friend and guest of Her Serene Highness, and I wish to be allowed to pass immediately."

"A friend of *His* Highness, perhaps," repeated the man thickly. "Or do you mean *girl*-friend? That's the good old English name, although in this country they call it *mistress*."

Catherine went scarlet.

"You – you!" she began and stopped, at a loss for further words.

He seized her arm again and held it in a vice-like grip.

"Don't get cross. I was only joking and personally I don't mind if His Highness does have a mistress or two. They all say he was a playboy when his father was alive, anyhow. But he's gone a bit holy. Anyhow, I like him. He's a good sort, and that's more than you can say for his bitch of a mother. I used to be on her staff. She liked a servant who could speak English as well as I do, to help with the English guests. But I drank too much wine and one day she kicked me out. Tonight I climbed over the wall. The sentries did not see me."

He laughed.

"They call me Johnny, down in my village. Mad Johnny. I'm always ready to do something crazy, I am. How about *you* being crazy with me tonight, *ma jolie fille*?"

Catherine began to panic. The perspiration broke out on her forehead. If she screamed, nobody would hear her – she had walked so far from Le Petit Palais. But she did not want to stay here and have a show-down with this man who admitted, himself, that he was a lunatic.

No, there was only one thing to do. Catherine was by no means helpless. She and Tom and one or two of their friends in her College had gone to Judo classes. Inspired, she thought with some irony, by that girl, Diana Rigg, in 'The Avengers'. At Oxford the girls used to wear black trousers and sweaters. They had an amusing as well as an instructive time. Kid-stuff, perhaps, but now Catherine couldn't be more thankful.

She started to walk away. The man came up behind her as she expected. The moment she felt his hands on her – he had clasped them about her throat – she kicked violently at his shins. He stepped back and she swiftly bent down and threw him. Slim though she was, she was strong, and using Judo methods a girl could throw the heaviest man if she knew how. 'Mad Johnny' went down with a roar of rage and pain, his head striking the stone paving that was laid around the Folly.

Catherine took to her heels and ran. She had winded Johnny but not knocked him out. She could hear him shouting, chasing after her. Her blood was up. She was going to win this round if she died for it, she thought. She wasn't going to feel his filthy hands on her again. She ran and ran and half-way through the Italian garden she came face to face with Dominic. The young Prince himself was taking a final night stroll, with one of his mother's wolfhounds at his heels. As Catherine more or less fell against him, he caught and steadied her. He threw a command over his shoulder to the dog.

"Sit down, Maxie. *Sit!* . . ."

Then to the girl he said:

"Catherine. *Pour l'amour de dieu*, what are you doing out here alone? What has happened? Who has frightened you? You look pale as death."

She gave a weak laugh and brushed her hair out of her eyes.

"There was a man . . . down there . . . by your Folly. I think he's crazy. Here he comes. Oh, *Dominic!*"

The Prince put her behind him and seized the wolfhound's collar.

"We will soon tackle him, Maxie and I. Did he attack you, Catherine?"

"In a way, yes," she gasped. "I think he's quite mad."

"Go back into the palace."

"No," she said. "No. I've had lessons in Judo. I threw him."

"You threw a man like that? I am flabbergasted," exclaimed Dominic.

'Mad Johnny' had reached them and stopped. He stood swaying, rubbing the back of his head. His eyes glared in the moonlight. Dominic approached him. He spoke rapidly to the man, who answered him; but Catherine did not understand what they said because they used the dialect of the Island. Then she saw the big yellow-haired man cringe away from the dog who was snapping the air with his teeth, looking decidedly unfriendly.

Dominic looked over his shoulder at Catherine.

"Of course, I know who this fellow is. He was once one of my mother's footmen whom she dismissed. I will stay here with him. He will not dare move, because he is afraid of Maxie. Please go and call one of the Guard, Catherine —"

Suddenly Catherine felt stupidly sorry for the crazy man who was blubbering like a baby, mixing French with English, begging for mercy.

"Honestly, I think he's crazy, Dominic. Don't send him to prison. He needs medical attention."

"My dear," said Dominic with a short laugh, "if he's crazy it is because he is never sober. Everybody on the Island knows him. He is a rogue and he is about due to be locked up."

"But he loves you, Dominic," said Catherine, feeling a quite ridiculous wish to save the brute who had just terrified her. Feeling, perhaps, merciful because she had beaten him.

"What do you mean—that he loves me?" demanded Dominic, astonished.

"He told me you were a good sort. He obviously likes his Prince."

"Well, he has a queer way of showing it, breaking into the grounds of my palace and frightening my most honoured guest."

"Perhaps he was drinking your health because on Saturday it is your birthday."

For a moment Dominic looked startled, then the anger

he had been feeling dissolved and his handsome features relaxed into a smile.

"You have a kind heart, Catherine."

"I beg the lady's pardon – I beg it, I beg *your* forgiveness, my Prince," moaned the man, and grovelled on the ground.

Catherine's quick gaze noted a trickle of blood running down his forehead. *She* had done that. He must have come a nasty crack against that stone.

"Can he not be taken to your hospital and receive psychiatric treatment?" she begged the Prince.

"Is that what you wish?"

"It would be wonderful as you are his Prince and in the position to save him from imprisonment," she murmured.

"You are very charming and romantic, Catherine."

"I resent that – romantic, indeed, after I've thrown six foot of hulking male," she protested indignantly.

"Very well," said Dominic. "I will do as you ask." He turned and spoke to the man who sprang on to his feet, overwhelmed with relief.

"You are a good sort, my Prince, a good sort, as I told the lady. I did not mean to frighten her, I had no idea she was an honoured guest. I will never come near the palace again, Your Highness, never."

"You will not be given the chance. You shall go to the psychiatric ward in our best hospital."

But Johnny suddenly turned and began to run as fast as his legs would carry him into the shadow of the cedar woods. He shouted as he went:

"Ah-ha – no hospital for me but he is a good sort, my Prince. Ah-ha! Long live Prince Dominic of Montracine!"

They heard his idiotic voice echoing through the stillness of the night. Dominic turned and looked down at Catherine. She drew a nervous breath.

"Well, that's that," she said. "You'll never catch him now, will you?"

Dominic looked at her and she looked back at him. They both burst out laughing.

"Well, *really, mon dieu!*" exclaimed Dominic. "This is a programme I had not arranged for you, Catherine. I do most humbly apologise for the crazy fellow."

"In retrospect, it has been quite thrilling. I was glad to find that the lessons I learned from one of our expert Judo teachers were not altogether wasted."

"You are as courageous as you are beautiful," he said. Then he began to laugh again and added, "Would you throw me in such a way and break my skull if I tried to lay a hand on you?"

Catherine, forgetting decorum, court etiquette, or the royal status of this young man, was flippant with him now.

"Shall I try, sir?"

"What!" he exclaimed. "You would like to do me an injury – this Prince who is such a good sort? Oh *really*; the thought of that crazy fellow may amuse me now, but I hope the rest of my loyal subjects are not all crazy, or is the whole world crazy tonight, my ter-rifically beautiful, brave Catherine?"

The wolfhound, free now from his restraining hand stretched himself out on the grass and began to chew playfully at a piece of wood.

Dominic looked down at Catherine who had not spoken again. Her eyes, he thought, were truly like glittering emeralds in the Mediterranean moonlight. He had not expected to find her here, so late at night, but she had been foremost in his mind when he began to take his stroll with the wolfhound.

The white coat had slipped from her shoulders. She was wearing the short black and white chiffon dress with the long transparent sleeves and charming ruffles around the wrists, that he had admired at dinner. He stared at her, as though fascinated. With her disordered hair and flushed cheeks she looked madly attractive, he thought. And suddenly the May moonlight and the enchantment of being alone with her away from etiquette – just the two of them, like any ordinary man and woman – any boy and girl – went to Dominic's head, like intoxicating wine.

He moved slowly towards her. She stood transfixed, looking up into his face. Those dark, almost tragic eyes of his were filled with an immense tenderness and longing. He put both hands on her shoulders and whispered her name:

"Catherine . . . *Catherine!*"

She could not speak, but the sweetness of that moment seemed to make an indelible mark on her life. A life that could never be the same again as she felt his arms around her, drawing her against him, and his lips on her mouth. Tenderness had become passion, longing was expressed in the warmth of that long-sustained kiss. They clung together feverishly in absolute silence. He kissed not only her lips but her cheeks and her closed eyes with the soft dark lashes. He threaded his fingers through her hair and kissed her forehead, her fine crescent brows – then her warm, responsive mouth again.

To Catherine, this love-making was a wonder and a delight. She had never dreamed that love could be like this but she did at least understand now why she had never before felt able to give her heart to any other man who had tried to make love to her. She responded to Dominic's caresses with all the fervour of her youth, knowing she was all his – not only in this moment – but for ever. She felt like an instrument answering and reverberating to the touch of his long fine fingers – to every exquisite caress. Then at last he drew away from her, seizing her hands, pressing each one to his lips. After what seemed to Catherine a whole lifetime of ecstasy, he let her go. She pushed her hair in that nervous way, back from her face. She still seemed unable to say one word but just shook her head incredulously as though she could not believe what had been taking place. Her lips burned and stung from his long delirious kisses. Her whole body felt as though it was on fire.

That he, too, was singularly shaken, she could see. In some curious way his whole expression had altered. Perhaps he lived usually behind a mask, she thought, because it was his destiny as a prince to rule, and to live only for his country and his people. But the man – the ordinary human being, no different from any of his people – was uppermost tonight. He spoke to her with a burning sincerity.

"I love you, Catherine," he said, "I love you with all my heart and soul. Now I know why I have waited so long – it was for you."

She stammered:

"I've been waiting for you, too."

"*Bien-aimée,*" he said in French. "*Ma douce chérie. Catherine. Mon amour.*"

She said:

"But of course this – is incredible – impossible. We mustn't love each other."

"You cannot tell me to stop loving you," he said with that sweet quick smile that made him look so youthful. "I just know that you are the one and only woman in the world for me."

She put both hands to her hot cheeks.

"But it *isn't* possible, Dominic – you know it isn't," she whispered.

"My darling, just because I am the Prince of Montracine and you are Miss Leigh-Holmes cannot alter the fact that I love you—and that you love me. You do, do you not, Catherine?"

"Yes, yes, Dominic."

He closed his eyes.

"I knew it from the beginning, my darling," he spoke in English.

"I did, too, Dominic."

"Then there is no more to be said."

She was exalted, enchanted—frightened by the whole affair. In unutterable confusion of mind, she shook her head and tried without success to keep a sense of proportion. The whole thing had happened so quickly and unexpectedly, she could hardly analyse the significance of it. But she did at least realise that there could never be an ordinary, happy love affair between herself and this man with his royal destiny.

She opened her lips as though to speak but Dominic held out his arms.

"Catherine," he said softly.

Like one bewitched, she went straight into those arms and curled her own around his neck and once again experienced the absolute sweetness and passion of his kisses. He seemed insatiable for her caresses and she responded warmly. So they stood there in the brilliance of that starlit night as though they felt safe together in the heart of a troubled world. Safe and ecstatically happy. Like this in each other's arms they could not look at the future but only live in the present in the first abandonment of their mutual desire.

But the moment had to come when the danger signal warned Dominic that however much he loved and wanted this girl, he must remember his position and particularly hers. In a crazy world when morals were becoming hopelessly distorted, even lost—and physical passion was indulged in lightly and thoughtlessly – he was still a prince, a man of particular honour. And this young English girl was his guest – the guest of Montracine.

He passed a hand over the richness of her hair.

"Catherine, sweet, beautiful Catherine, we cannot discuss anything fully tonight – there is no time. We must go back."

"Yes, yes, I agree."

"I will take you straight to the palace but you must go in alone. We must not let anybody see us together. This is for your reputation's sake, not mine."

"I understand," she nodded, and reflected that he knew only too well that his mother had her spies and used them.

"You understand, do you not," he went on, "that if I could, I would stay out in this enchanted garden all night long with you. I am so much in love, Catherine."

He was so direct, so simple and even naïve about his feelings for her. She was deeply touched.

"Oh, Dominic, I can't help loving you!" she said.

Her eyes were marvellous, he thought, and there seemed a new beauty in them in this hour – a greater depth. He could hardly bear not to pull her back into his arms, carry her into the little 'Folly' and keep her in there.

"Catherine," he said. "Somehow we have to get through tomorrow's programme with a palace full of people, then there will be my birthday celebration. After that, we will seriously discuss our situation."

"I thought my father and I were leaving the day after –" she began.

"No, you must stay longer," he said imperiously. This brought her down to earth, reminding her that even if Dominic wanted to play the lover he was still conscious of his position. Yet she realised that he was afraid of his own ardour. That was flattering to her.

"I only want to ask you one question before we say

good-night," he said. "Have you ever loved any other man – I mean – as you love me?"

"Never."

"But you must have been approached by many – at Oxford – in Paris —"

"Of course most girls have the odd affair – who doesn't? But I've never kissed any man on earth as I kissed you just now."

There was a long silence. Then Dominic inclined his head.

"I am deeply honoured, my Catherine."

She thought: *What a darling – what an absolute honey he is and oh, my God, how terribly I love him. But it can never never come to anything, no matter what he says to me in two days' time.*

He turned to the wolfhound who rose, wagging his tail, and followed at his heels as he escorted Catherine to the wrought-iron gates opening into the Italian garden. There he took her hand and kissed it lingeringly.

"Good-night, my Love," he whispered. "The next forty-eight hours will be difficult, because all I want to do is to be with you. I may not be able to see you alone at all. But please *know* that I love you. Be with me in spirit, Catherine."

"I will – I am now. I'll always be with you in spirit," she said breathlessly, turned and walked quickly up the steps on to the terrace and into the palace. She felt, as she walked through the long, splendid corridors, that she was in some crazy wonderful dream – a dream from which she must eventually awaken. And this was the tragedy.

10

"Well, Pop, how do I look?"

Edward Leigh-Holmes who had been brushing a sleeve, turned and looked at his daughter, who had just knocked and entered the dressing-room.

He knew when he heard that word 'Pop' that Catherine was in a mood of excitement. He wasn't surprised. This was an exciting day for her – a day for any young English girl to remember. Few were privileged to be a guest in the palace of a reigning prince on what the French called his '*Anniversaire*'.

Clothes-brush suspended in one hand, Mr. Leigh-Holmes said:

"Phew!" He whistled and his aesthetic and often severe face broke into a smile. "Very snazzy, darling."

"So you think I'm okay?"

"Indeed yes, and very like your mother today. I know the fashions were different when she was with me on gala occasions, but you have her figure exactly. Different colouring – but your lips – your smile – that little shy way of looking through your lashes when you *know* how attractive you are – those are hers. Time rolls back for me, Catherine!"

"I'm glad," said the girl, "and only wish for your sake, darling Daddy, that Mum was with us now."

Mr. Leigh-Holmes went on looking at her wistfully, tenderly. They were both dressed, ready for the *déjeuner* which was to be held today in the big dining hall at half-past one. There would be thirty or forty people at this palace banquet after the March-Past of the Prince's troops.

All the women would be wearing long dresses, and hats; the men in uniform if they were in the Services, or like Mr. Leigh-Holmes, in morning-coat and striped trousers.

"We might be going to Ascot," Mr. Leigh-Holmes added, smiling.

Said Catherine:

"You said I was looking through my lashes, Daddy. That makes me sound horribly coquettish."

"I could never accuse you of being a coquette, Kate," he smiled. "Especially not since you told me about your little Judo session with that crazy chap the night before last."

Catherine lapsed into silence. *The night before last*. If only Daddy knew exactly what had happened down there outside the white temple in the blaze of moonlight, but nobody knew and she had been hugging the intoxicating secret to herself ever since it happened.

Somehow she had managed to get through yesterday's formalities knowing that *he* was having to get through them too. They had exchanged only the briefest glances, and a few formal or friendly words, according to who was near by. Le Petit Palais had filled up since the first plane landed at Montracine Airport, and the first Hovercraft arrived from the mainland soon after the *petit déjeuner*.

Catherine had been introduced to so many people, she could only remember a few of the most striking. Among them one or two representatives of Spain, of Greece, of West Germany, and the Far East. An exquisite almond-eyed Asian Princess; a Maharajah with a wife wearing a fabulous sari; all staying here as guests of the Prince.

Apart from the diplomatic crowd there were relations, of

course. The Marquise Louise de Courbese, widowed aunt of the Prince, and her daughters Françoise and Clarisse, the Vicomte du Balençons and his wife, first cousins; the Marchesa Caraletto – a handsome black-haired Italian, sister of Isabella. Catherine had heard the Princesse call her Térèsa; other names she could not really remember. There had been a huge gathering last night. It had been quite interesting. But Catherine had been utterly bored, wanting desperately to be with *him*, able sadly, only to watch him in the crowd.

Just for an instant, when she said good-night, Dominic managed to whisper a few words in her ear. He had manœuvred things so that he was standing beside the door as she neared it. Her father had stayed behind to say a word to one of his diplomatic friends. Dominic looked down at Catherine and bowed formally. But his eyes had not been formal, and her whole body had sprung to life – glowing and happy again.

"Good-night, my love," he whispered, "I look upon this instant as the most precious of the day. Remember Omar Khayyám's words:

> '*One moment in annihilation's waste . . .*
> *One moment of the well of life to taste . . .*'"

She said softly:

"Fitzgerald's beautiful translation of *The Rubá'iyát.*"

There had been no time for him to say any more because a footman had sprung forward, and all she could do was to look at Dominic hoping that he would read all that she felt – that she wanted to say.

This morning awake in the early hours, she had thought: *This is the day on which he was born. Born to be a Prince. Oh, God, I love him so much. I wish he were just plain Mr.*

Smith or Mr. Anything, without a penny in the world. I wish we could have the right just to get into his little, littlest car, and drive away to the other side of the world – alone.

But she had realised that this was all romantic nonsense – wishful thinking – and that the sooner she steeled herself against her emotions the better. She accused herself of being out of her mind even to think of Dominic in such intimate terms. Yet he had kissed her. He had told her he loved her. Where now was the old sensible Catherine who used not to deny that such love existed and that one day she would fall in love and marry, but who had scoffed at anything approaching *this* sort of sentimental indulgence.

She and her father had brought a small gift for Dominic from London, knowing that they would be here for his birthday. At the time it had seemed appropriate and Daddy had been generous. They had found something essentially English – an engraving of Victorian London: St. Paul's Cathedral with snow on the ground and a cloudy sky, beautifully framed in black and gold.

"I think he will appreciate it as he loves London," Mr. Leigh-Holmes had said, "and it is a particularly fine engraving."

Now when she thought of it, it seemed a humble gift. Catherine wished it had been much, *much* more wonderful. Yet she knew there was little she could give *him* which he had not already got in this beautiful palace full of wonderful things. She had suddenly heard the sound of cannon fire while she drank her breakfast coffee. The little Montracine army, honouring their Prince, firing from the Square of their barracks. Twenty-six volleys shattering the peace of the morning.

Catherine had rushed to open the jalousies. She stepped into a blaze of sunshine to listen to the last few rounds although she could see nothing but the gold-misted morning, the blue sky and the blue, blue sea far below the hill.

Then she had gone back to her bed and whispered in the silence of her room:

"Happy Birthday to you, Dominic, darling *Dominic*."

Even now she felt quite unable to speak his name aloud and think of him with such familiarity and not feel that she was being impudent. For who was Catherine Leigh-Holmes to behave as though the Prince of Montracine had become a 'boy-friend', like any other?

She did not see Dominic to speak to during that morning, although afterwards he told her how difficult he had found it not to betray himself by sending her a message and special flowers. But things like that he was unable to do in the palace, teeming with people.

Until midday Catherine went out with her father. They drove down to the Port and walked around.

Every street was gay with fluttering pennants and bright coloured flags. Shops were closed but cafés open. Crowds were gathering round the fountain in the Square. In the harbour, all the boats were beflagged. The ceaseless sound of music came from hundreds of homes. There were many bright banners hanging out, bearing gilded inscriptions.

VIVE LE PRINCE–DOMINIC IV. BONNE ANNIVERSAIRE!

Most of the populace turned out on foot, but there were many vehicles (collected from the past), jostling in the roadways. Donkey-carts and wagons pulled by fat country ponies, their shaggy manes plaited, and beribboned.

Farmers and their wives, men and women of all ages and from every kind of shop and factory linked arms, five and six abreast, and danced round the Square singing songs in the patois that Catherine could not understand. But continually she heard the words: "*Vive le Prince.*"

She began to feel a warmth and a pride in this manifestation of homage from so many Montracineans. A warmth and a pride, for *him*.

Once when she looked up at a gay little house with wrought-iron balconies, festooned with flowers – a young man called down to her and blew her a kiss.

"*Jolie mademoiselle. Vous êtes mignonne!*" he called to her.

She laughed and waved back. At least she understood that he thought her attractive. Gradually the excitement, the friendliness, the joy that the islanders were showing in the celebration of their ruler's birthday, woke an answering chord in her. She must not be sad or silent because circumstances separated her from Dominic today. It was *his* day. She must join with all the others in being gay.

"It's fun, isn't it? Aren't you glad you came, darling?" her father murmured while they strolled down to the harbour and watched one of the new Hovercraft plunging through the water, throwing up a great cloud of silvery foam.

"It's terrific," she said.

But she was pursued by the memory of the night before last.

"*I love you, Catherine,*" he had said.

To herself she kept saying:

It isn't true. I've dreamed it up. It can't have happened.

Yet she felt completely removed from the former mundane life that she lived in the solemn little house in London.

Now, facing her father in his dressing-room, she was tense and uncertain of her feelings. Things were made no better by the memory of Dominic's mother last night on the one occasion when Her Serene Highness had deigned to speak to the least of her guests. Isabella had seemed cool and unapproachable. Catherine did not think she was wrong in suspecting that the Princesse resented her presence here. And undoubtedly she had been scandalised when she had learned through Leveuve that Catherine had joined the Prince at the swimming-pool.

"Well," she heard her father's voice, "are you ready to go, darling?"

Catherine gathered her thoughts together. She threw a final look at herself in the mirror.

Yes, the dress definitely suited her. It was her colour . . . a rich shade of green transparent material with a pattern of huge smoke-grey flowers. As sleeveless and low-necked and long as an evening dress, it was caught at her slim waist with a silver belt. She wore long green gloves and a large hat of transparent tulle, the brim curving back from her forehead, showing a strand of chestnut hair. Her lashes were dark and her eyelids a delicate mauve. Her eyes looked enormous; her lips delicately pink. Yes, she had to admit frankly that she had never looked more beguiling.

Which man shall I beguile? she asked herself with a sudden laugh: *Leveuve or the frightful Reynard—the crafty Fox? I hate them both. I am sure they are both spies, in Isabella's pay;* against *him.* I wish I could tell him to be more careful of them.

On the other hand she really knew nothing about it and had not the least right to express such suspicions.

"Come along, Glamour-girl," said her father. "You're day-dreaming."

He was right, she thought. And a moment later, with the other privileged guests they were on a raised platform under the awning outside Le Petit Palais to watch the March-Past of His Serene Highness's troops. Catherine had brought her Leica camera with her and took several shots of the display.

Her gaze turned to Dominic – standing on his own dais, a central figure in white dress uniform with the gold epaulettes on his shoulders, and decorations glittering in the sun. Just behind him stood Isabella of Montracine. She, too, was in white, forsaking her usual black – a long white lace dress; a small hat on her dark head with a white ostrich feather curling down to her neck. She looked handsome and regal, *and* arrogant, Catherine thought, then reproached herself for being prejudiced. But somehow she could not feel any real warmth towards Dominic's mother.

Dominic raised a hand and stood at the salute. Catherine might have been amused by the sight of what her English friends would call 'the toy army' as the young soldiers in their country's uniform stepped smartly by, led by nice-looking officers with their flashing swords unsheathed.

Every head turned now towards the figure of the young man on the dais. A military band played a stirring march. The flags fluttered and the crowd who had been allowed to pour into the palace grounds to see this sight, waved and cheered. Children, some held on the shoulders of their fathers, held up tiny flags.

There followed the cavalry. Montracine had not yet exchanged all its horses for armoured cars, although there was a squadron of armoured vehicles, and of course a small naval contingent in white drill – for Montracine boasted a couple of warships – and then, the bright blue uniforms of the officers and men of the Montracine Air Force.

It was small. It was charming, Catherine thought enthusiastically. It was even impressive in its way. Suddenly she, who had always prided herself on being a bit of a realist, felt the sting of tears behind her eyelids and a lump in her throat. The tears literally blinded her as she looked again at the young Prince – standing there so erect, so regal, with his gloved hand at the salute.

Oh, my darling, she thought, and wondered why she felt a sudden anguish, *Oh, my darling!*

Then with the body of Palace Guards bringing up the rear, the March-Past ended.

Everybody relaxed but a roar went up from the crowd to the accompaniment of a volley of several guns down the hill synchronised to make this moment more stirring.

"*Vive le Prince! Bonne Anniversaire!*"

The crics echoed through the exotic grounds. The date-palms waved gently in the breeze. The sun beat down from a cloudless cobalt sky. For the first time Catherine heard cries from the throats of the Italians – distinctive, perhaps not as frenzied:

"*Viva! Viva!*" they shouted. A few voices – Catherine noted somehow with satisfaction, only a *very* few – cried "*Viva La Princesse Isabella!*"

She saw Dominic's mother wave and smile, then turn to chat vivaciously with her son who had come to her side. Suddenly Catherine felt insignificant and alone, and although there was not a man young or old who had not glanced at her twice with open continental flattery, she felt not an atom of pleasure or vanity. She made a sudden excuse to her father, slipped away from the guests who were all talking and gossiping together in little circles, and went into the palace.

Somehow she needed the silence and the darkness, yet even in the cool, marble hall her face burned hotly and she fancied she could hear the beating of her own passionate heart.

I shall run away, she thought, crazily, *I must get away from here and from him.*

Then she felt her father's gentle hand on her shoulder.

"What is it, darling?"

At the sound of that loved voice which had so often

comforted her when she was a child and guided her as she grew older, she turned and choked a little, handkerchief pressed against her lips.

"Sorry, Daddy, I'm an imbecile. I – I'll be all right in a moment."

He gazed at her sadly. She was pale now and looked so unhappy that it both startled and troubled Edward Leigh-Holmes. But he did not voice what he thought. He said quietly:

"That's all right, sweetie. It's just a touch of the sun I wouldn't wonder. Over-excitement, or, have you been greedy and eaten too much rich French food?"

She dabbed at her lips, and giggled.

"That's it. You know me; old Greedy Guts! But I'm fine now. Let's go back."

"Good girl," he said.

So Catherine returned to the crowds, to the chattering and the exercising of her best French, and even spoke a smattering of Italian to the Princesse's various relatives and friends.

Only once did she feel close to Dominic that day. That was when his dark mesmeric eyes caught the full glance of hers as they all sat down to the banquet at the long glittering tables. She was not very near him but near enough to see that long meaning look. Suddenly all her depression and stupidity rolled away. What his eyes said to her seemed as eloquent as spoken words. It was as though a flame glowed between them. And even when he looked away and began to talk to the old Marchesa who was on his right – she still felt the warmth and thrill of the flame and she knew that she could not take one step away from Montracine – not one, in case it removed her from the sight of him for ever.

11

So passed that difficult day. Catherine tried to rest during the siesta hour when the guests were in their own rooms and there fell a silence and lazy languor over Le Petit Palais.

Soon came the evening celebrations—the carnival. The royal guests with the Prince and his mother heading the procession, drove through the streets to watch the fun and the feasting.

In the main Square crowds were still dancing, shouting and cheering. Little cars and peasant carts, gay with streamers and flowers, continued to pass through the streets in a never-ending stream. Many of the young people were masked at this hour and wore carnival costumes and caps. Overhead the sky was one great canopy of stars. As soon as the Rolls Royce was sighted there were cries of "*Vive le Prince!*" in touching loyalty to their young ruler. Every balcony was packed with onlookers singing and throwing streamers or confetti into the streets.

Then came the fireworks. Glittering whirling golden circles of the Catherine wheels, swift uprising rockets, the whiz-bang of bombs that exploded high in the air and came down in stars into a silver moon-mirrored sea. The flickering fitful showers from the hundreds of sparklers carried by screaming excited children lit up their happy faces.

In the car driving with Catherine and her father were two young French cousins of Dominic's, both of whom spoke excellent English. Catherine was as young and as gay as any of them. Hatless, her hair tumbled about her shoulders, she looked a teenager still, her father thought, even tonight in her long elegant dress. How much he loved her! She had been everything to him since her mother died. What a terrible calamity it would be if she were to fall seriously in love with Prince Dominic. Their ways lay hopelessly apart. It could bring her nothing but pain.

But pain for the moment was dormant in Catherine's heart and she applauded as she watched the fireworks, and threw back streamers and flowers when they were flung at her. Then suddenly the accident happened. A young sailor, a little tipsy with the wine that had been flowing all day, looked at the beautiful girl with her wonderful eyes and rich flowing hair and shouting "*Belle Fille!*" threw a shower of sparklers at her, meant for her lap. Instead, they caught the delicate inflammable material of one wide organza sleeve. In a second she became a bright human torch, screaming, terror-stricken, beating at the air.

It could have been serious. She was saved by her father who flung himself upon her, rolling her over in the back seat of the car while Dominic's young French cousins stood up, clutching each other in panic.

Within seconds, Mr. Leigh-Holmes had extinguished the flames. The sailor ran away, sober and frightened by what he had done. A crowd gathered round, hemming in the car. There were murmurs of sympathy and horror and as the story spread from mouth to mouth, the Square became suddenly quieter.

Catherine remembered little about that accident because after the first horror of the burning organza, she was stifled by her father's weight and bruised by the way his hands beat against her, putting out the flames. She fainted.

She did not see the Rolls which had been heading the Palace procession come to a standstill, nor the figure of the

Prince, himself, running towards the Leigh-Holmes car. He had only just heard that a young English girl had been injured, and that her dress was ablaze. At once he had guessed it must be Catherine. *His Catherine!* When first he had risen, and begun to open the door of the Rolls, he had felt his mother clutch at his hand. He heard her hissing whisper:

"Dominic, *Dio mio*—do not go to her! There is no need. . . ."

But he leapt out of the car and ran. He stared in utter dismay at the sight of Catherine lying against her father, unconscious. The upper part of her dress was scorched, blackened, full of jagged holes. There was an acrid odour of burning material in the air. The young French cousins were still clinging together, weeping in sympathy.

Mr. Leigh-Holmes looked deeply shaken.

"It's all right, sir . . . thank God she is not badly hurt."

"But she is burned!" exclaimed Dominic with horror in his voice, and pointed to a big patch of blistered skin on Catherine's right shoulder. There were more angry patches on her neck, and two black marks spoiling the smooth curve of her cheek.

Dominic looked at her in utter consternation.

"*Mon Dieu!*" he muttered. "Who has done this? The police shall find the idiot responsible and —"

"No, no, sir, it was a pure accident," broke in Mr. Leigh-Holmes. "A silly drunk who meant no real harm, I am sure. Catherine would not want any fuss. If you could just give orders for a passage to be cleared so that the chauffeur can get us back to the palace —" Mr. Leigh-Holmes paused. He had seen more than a normal concern in the young Prince's eyes and suddenly, instinctively, he picked up Catherine's short transparent coat which was on her lap and covered her almost naked breasts. Then the girl opened her eyes.

The first thing she saw was Dominic's beloved face bent close to hers, and the horror in his eyes.

She smiled faintly.

"Oh hello . . . I . . . Dominic . . ." she broke off and sat up. She was shivering and feverish; more shocked than hurt, for none of her burns was serious owing to her father's timely action. Then swiftly she became conscious of her position, remembered what had happened and was more than a little perturbed to see that the Prince had left his own car and come to hers.

"Thank you for your concern, sir," she said in a loud clear voice, wanting for his sake to prevent any whisper of scandal.

Dominic had the hardest task not to pull her into his arms and kiss that lovely face with the scorch marks from brow to chin; to hold and to comfort her and tell her that any hurt she felt, he must feel too, and that anything that happened to her in this life must and would always affect him vitally. There were no two doubts about that in his mind now.

But he had to pull himself together and remember his position, and the fact that he was the cynosure of all eyes. The Leigh-Holmes' car was besieged by a gaping inquisitive crowd.

He stepped back from Catherine and shut the door.

"Thanks be to God," he said in French. "No real harm has been done. Mademoiselle is quite all right."

At that precise moment, the Chief of the Montracine Police arrived in his jeep preceded by three motor-bikes, their sirens screaming, scattering the crowd to the right and the left.

"Are you really all right, my darling?" Catherine's father asked her.

A sympathetic bystander thrust a half-filled bottle of

wine into his hand. Mr. Leigh-Holmes uncorked it, soaked his handkerchief in the *vin-du-pays* and dabbed at Catherine's temples. She recovered her sense of humour and laughed weakly:

"Don't waste it, Pop, give me a drink."

After that he knew that she was all right.

Dominic had gone. One word from him and the Chief of Police bowed from the waist, saluted and now begged Mr. Leigh-Holmes to allow him to escort them back to Le Petit Palais. He and his men would ensure that they got there without delay, so that *la pauvre Mademoiselle* could see the doctor at once.

And that, for Catherine, was the end of the carnival, and of Dominic's birthday.

She did not attend the evening supper-party. She wanted to go but her father forbade it. One of the Princesse's Italian staff, who had had hospital training was sent by Her Serene Highness to attend the young English lady until the palace doctor arrived.

Catherine, much against her will, found herself in bed doing as she was told by the voluble Italian woman who made more of the injuries than she need do, with much rolling of the eyes and gesticulating, and praising of *le bon Dieu* who had saved Mademoiselle's life.

Catherine felt like saying 'Don't be so stupid. My life was never in danger, and I am just a bit scorched. The blisters will soon go down if they are properly treated. I am very healthy and I heal quickly.'

But she had to admit she was glad when it was all over and the doctor had been, dressed the blisters and gone again. Then after a drink she was alone and quiet again in her bedroom.

What a to-do! What a wretched thing to have happened, she reflected, and how wonderful *he* had been to come to her like that. Wonderful if, perhaps, tactless. Heaven knew what his mother must think. It would certainly be a good thing when the Leigh-Holmes left Montracine, she told herself wryly.

It was neither the throbbing of her head nor the pain of her blisters that kept her from sleeping; it was the memory of Dominic. She lay with closed eyes, listening to the faint sound of fireworks and music. She re-lived that moment when she had opened her eyes and seen Dominic's, so dark, so tender, so concerned, looking down at her.

Despite the sedative the doctor had given her, her mind seemed to remain alert. She began to feel hot and feverish again, twisting, turning, throwing off all the bedclothes, although the night air coming through the slats of the jalousies was cool.

She did not know what time it was – it seemed long ago since her father had looked in to ask how she was and to kiss her good-night. For no reason at all, except that she was still suffering from shock as well as the tenderness of the superficial burns, she began to cry.

Somebody knocked on the door.

"*Entrez,*" she said quickly, wiping her eyes.

An old woman dressed in black came in. Catherine recognised her, the old '*bonne*' who had helped the superior English nanny look after Dominic when he was young. She worshipped him and still held a place on the palace staff although she did nothing much but work in the linen room or knit.

She had spoken to Catherine once or twice, very respectfully after Dominic had introduced her.

"My old Augusta who was so kind to me."

And to the old woman: "You must meet my new English friend, Augusta."

Augusta tip-toed to the bedside and looked down at the

pink-flushed face of the young English lady. She seemed to her most beautiful with her long chestnut hair tossed over the pillow, and her big bright green eyes.

Augusta held up a white woolly monkey—a child's toy with a comical grin on its realistic little face. Catherine stared at it blinking.

"Oh, whatever is it, Augusta?" she asked in French.

The old woman explained haltingly, for she spoke patois rather than pure French. Cackling, laughing, she told Catherine that the monkey used to be His Serene Highness's favourite toy when he was in the nursery. He had loved it more than any of the much more expensive presents cramming the royal cupboards. When he was ill, suffering from some childish complaint, or the headache he used to get when he was small—he would ask for his little *babouin*. Augusta maintained that it had magic qualities and always cured him. Tonight after the celebrations were finished, she had gone to see His Highness, Augusta said. He had looked pale and drawn and troubled, walking up and down his room instead of undressing.

He was still her beloved child and when she had offered to bathe his temples with *eau de toilette*, he had refused. It was the English *demoiselle* about whom he was concerned, of that she was sure. He feared that she had been badly hurt because that idiot had thrown the firework. He was ordering a new dress to be sent to her from a shop in Monte Carlo tomorrow, and her room was to be filled with flowers. On and on, the old woman gabbled, Catherine only just able to translate. But there was no doubt as to the meaning of her final words when she thrust the monkey into Catherine's hands. Please to hold it tonight, Augusta begged—it would cure her—and Catherine did not laugh because she could see the old peasant, like all her kind, was genuinely superstitious.

"I comforted His Serene Highness, but I dared not tell him I was going to bring the *babouin* to you. He called it by the English name – *Monkey*. He used to fall asleep holding it in his little hands."

Her Serene Highness deplored such nonsense and had once or twice tried to get rid of the toy. But on the first occasion when the little Prince could not find it he had been so distressed, the Princesse had had to return it, although she had meant to throw it in the fire.

"You will see," the old woman ended, "tomorrow you will be well again, my Noble Lady."

Catherine, not knowing whether to call this rubbish or be moved by it, found herself clasping the shabby little white monkey against her breast as she thanked Augusta.

So *he* had held it, and it had comforted him when he was small.

How sweet, she thought, *how sweet and absurd.*

Then Augusta added that His Highness had told her to wish the Lady a good night's rest and to say he would pay her a visit in the morning.

"Please thank him, Augusta, and beg him not to send for another dress for me – he need not."

The old woman bowed as though Catherine herself was royalty, and walked out of the room.

Catherine turned off her lamp. The pure white Mediterranean moonlight slanted through the shutters. All was still now in Le Petit Palais. The Island festivities had ended.

She still held the woolly toy. Oh, how ridiculous, cried one half of her brain, but the other half was strangely soothed. This was *his* childhood's toy, preserved all these long years by the faithful old nurse. *His* mascot. Now it was hers, for the rest of the night.

"Oh, *petit babouin,*" she whispered, "you and I are going to be friends. I feel almost that you are real. Yet nothing else is real. All this is fantasy, and back I shall go in a day or two to London and my own realistic existence with both my feet planted firmly on the ground."

Her eyes began to close. To open – to close again – drowsily.

Before she knew where she was she was asleep.

The next time she awoke it was morning. A maid was pulling aside the shutters and letting in a little of the sunlight. Her breakfast table had already been wheeled in.

Quickly, Catherine hid the white monkey under the sheet, half-ashamed of the way she had cuddled it all night. Of course it was coincidence but she felt immeasurably better. Her various 'scorches' and blisters smarted a little, but her temperature was down. She sat up, stretching, curling her fingers. The maid came towards her, smiling.

"His Serene Highness has sent you these, Mam'selle," she said, and she handed Catherine a big silver bowl filled with violets. Hundreds of them she thought, purple and fragrant – fantastically beautiful with the dew still on them. Afterwards she learned that the head-gardener of the palace was famous throughout France as well as the Island for his violets.

"Oh, how exquisite!" she exclaimed, and touched the little flowers with her lips.

The maid put the bowl on the table beside her.

"Mam'selle is better?"

"Absolutely all right again – don't I look it?"

The little maid smiled as she nodded and examined the English *demoiselle's* beautiful face. It was hardly marked. Certainly on the creamy pallor of her shoulders there were pieces of lint that had been strapped there by the doctor with healing ointment. Otherwise she looked better as she said – much better than when she had arrived back last night, half-fainting.

Catherine waited until the girl had gone, then tore open the envelope that had been handed to her with the violets.

A note from Dominic:

"*Once again all my apologies. I am desolated that the accident should ever have happened. Forgive Montracine, and get well quickly and let me make amends. I will come to see you later if you will allow.*

Dominic."

Her pulses thrilled. She felt there must be stars in her eyes as she looked once again at the violets in the lovely silver bowl.

She was being treated like a member of the family, spoiled as she had never been in her life before. It embarrassed her a little, but to know that he was so concerned for her could only bring her joy.

When would he come, she asked herself, as she poured out her coffee. Would he come alone? No, that wouldn't be etiquette. Oh, when, *when* would she see him alone again – if ever? Had that hour of love down in the garden ever really been? Had he ever really said '*I love you*'?

Her father came in to share his breakfast with her and talk, delighted to find his Catherine restored.

Even from him she hid Dominic's little monkey, and dared not even suggest that the toy had supernatural powers of healing. But anyhow she felt gloriously alive – vividly alert this morning; longing, *longing* to see the Prince – *her* Prince, at least during that one hour.

When eventually she was alone and Dominic came she had put on the nylon and lace jacket that she seldom wore even when it was cold, at home. In a spirit of mischief she had seated the white monkey on the top of her pillow.

The expected knock came at the door soon after eleven. To

her utter surprise the Prince of Montracine walked in by himself.

After closing the door, he stood with his back against it – staring at her. He said:

"I cannot even begin to think what kind of scandal there would be if I were seen coming into your room like this. But I was careful. Nobody was in the corridor. I only mean to stay one moment."

With a fast-beating heart she returned his gaze.

"'*One moment in annihilation's waste?*'" she quoted.

His face looked suddenly radiant.

He answered:

"Yes – '*One moment of the well of life to taste*'."

Quickly he ran forward and bent on one knee beside her, raising her hand to his lips, a courtier rather than a prince.

"I have not slept all night – thinking of you and worrying about your accident. Oh, my *darling*, it nearly drove me mad when I saw you in that car. It was one of the most terrible moments of my life."

His exaggeration filled her with tenderness. He was so unlike an Englishman would have been in the circumstances. Emotional; perhaps too much so. She might have laughed about it if it had been anybody but the man she now loved with her whole heart and soul.

She felt his lips warm and passionate against the palms of both her hands.

"Catherine, *Catherine*, I love you so much."

"And I love you," she whispered. "Thank you, oh, so much for my gorgeous violets."

"I dare not stay. I dare not be found here alone with you," he said. "To us, it means nothing. We would be jeered at by young people of our age – ordinary people – for being so prim, so proper. But here, I am always in the limelight, and you have a reputation which I value highly."

"You're very sweet. But you mustn't kneel to me, please – somehow it seems quite wrong. I should be curtsying to you . . ." She added with a mixture of merriment and gravity: "*Your Serene Highness.*"

"Oh, nonsense!" he exclaimed.

That was so English that it made her burst out laughing. He laughed too. Then suddenly he saw the little toy on her pillow.

"Good heavens – how has my white monkey found his way to *you*?"

She reached up an arm which he found childishly youthful and slender, picked up the toy and handed it to him.

"Augusta told me that you would want it back. But your *babouin* has worked the miracle – I swear it. I'm not in pain any more and I feel so well I'm going to get up later on."

"My stupid little monkey – and you are not laughing at me! Oh, Catherine, really, you are ter-rific."

She held out her arms.

The next moment he was sitting on her bed and they clung together passionately. His hungry kisses were on her lips, her cheeks, her throat, and tenderly touched the injured shoulder.

"*Bien-aimée* . . . Well loved," he said and went on kissing her recklessly. It was she who grew acutely aware now of their perilous position. She pushed him away.

"You must go. You *must*, Dominic. You know that I want you to stay but you *must* not be found here."

But that was the moment when the Princesse Isabella of Montracine chose to pay a duty call upon the injured guest, bringing with her the wife of the present English Ambassador, Lady Daltry.

There was a knock. The Prince sprang to his feet but it was too late for him to make his escape. His mother walked briskly into the room, followed by Patricia Daltry who carried a gilt basket full of magnificent grapes.

For a moment complete silence fell. The acid-sweet smile Isabella had forced, froze on her lips when she found her son alone at Catherine's bedside. Pat Daltry, a woman with a sense of humour which had at times threatened to undermine her husband's dignity and importance, blinked and thought: *well – well – WELL!*

And Catherine, for the first time in her life was completely unable to move or speak but just sat there, her pulses racing, wondering what would happen next.

12

(Extract from a letter written by Catherine Leigh-Holmes on June 15th, to her cousin Belinda Holt):

"I've been at home with plenty to think about for the last fortnight and I wanted terribly to see you because you are the only person I've really confided in. Then James told me that you were spending a month with the twins down in Frinton with your Mum because of my god-child's tonsil operation. I do hope the poppet is better. So I'm typing this on my little machine. I just must get it off my chest. I'm in such a daze, Belinda. The only thing that keeps my feet firmly on the ground this morning is the fact that I'm back in Chester Square and it's cold after Montracine. I hope you're not having the same beastly weather by the sea.

Belinda, I'm terribly in love—and in such an awkward situation, you just don't KNOW. I really feel quite frantic. That's something for me. You think I am quiet and sensible, and complain that it is you who have nerves. Well, my goodness, I've got them now . . ."

Sitting in her bedroom, typing on the little table where she used to work in the vacs. when she was at Oxford, Catherine scanned through the three sheets already typed. There were plenty of errors but she just didn't care. She had rushed on at speed, as she always did. Belinda would understand—dear plump Belinda, attractive if not pretty, and so much to be envied with her adoring husband and those gorgeous twins. Ever since she married her doctor – James Holt – Catherine had lined her up among the truly 'happy-marrieds'. Often told her that she, herself, would probably be less lucky. Belinda used to laugh and assure her her turn would come.

And it has come with a vengeance, Catherine reflected, *only I'm hardly a 'happy-married'.*

She skipped through the part about her original meeting with Dominic followed by the gradual development of love between them, then described the visit to the Island.

"I can't say I was feeling a hundred per cent that morning after the birthday fête when everything blew up. Patricia Daltry – we call her Lady D. at home; she's a nice cosy person – couldn't have been more tactful. I think she summed up the situation. She just behaved as though it was natural to find His Serene Highness in my bedroom. She chatted to us both, sympathised about my being burnt, etc., then pushed off which was awful because I was left alone with HER. As I've already told you I reckon the Dowager Princesse is one of the most venomous women alive, a serpent behind that devilish sweetness and courtesy she exhibits to the world. But she wasn't very sweet to me that morning once Pat left. In a voice like cracked ice she told Dominic she wished to talk to him on urgent business, asked me politely how I was, then marched out of the room. I assure you, Belinda, the sugar-pink roses she had handed me might have been Deadly Nightshade. Dominic just gave me one of those heart-shaking looks from those marvellous eyes of his and followed Maman. I suppose he has to knuckle down to her because she has always held such a position of authority and the Montracine people make sort of matriarchal goddesses out of their mothers. Anyhow I thought the best thing I

could do was to leave this Island as quickly as possible. You know how terrific Daddy can be and he couldn't have been more understanding when I told him about the faux-pas *and Her Serene Highness's reactions. I suggested we should get going and say he wished me to see some big plastic surgeon in London about the worst of the scars on my neck. A mere nothing, mind you, but we could make it our excuse.*

I don't know what sort of flare-up there was between mother and son, but there must have been one because after I got up and was finishing my packing, a note came from Dominic saying that he wished me to see him immediately in his private writing-room.

I went down with a chiffon scarf over my hair which had been ruined by the accident, and carrying my gloves and bag just to prove that I meant to go.

I found Dominic alone. Poor darling! He looked so grim and rather pallid. He just took me in his arms and told me that he had told HER I was the only girl for him and that he intended to marry me. When she said that he must be out of his mind, and hardly knew me, etc. etc, he apparently stuck to his guns. I don't know why, Belinda, I feel quite bouleversée and unable to rationalise my feelings but I do know it IS a real thing between Dominic and myself. No matter whether he's a ruling Prince and I'm a commoner, or not. He said he had told his mother that she had always wanted him to marry and settle down and have children so now she had got her way. But it was no use her pushing Sophie d'Arlennes or anyone else of her choice at him. Neither did it matter whether he had known me for four days or four years, he still intended with, Daddy's permission, to ask me to marry him.

Of course I was flabbergasted. We'd had a romantic session and he'd said he was in love with me but I didn't think it was altogether serious. I only know I'd marry him if he turned out to be a penniless nobody, and you know me, Belinda, I'm no seeker after cash or high places. Certainly I'm not a snob and my best friends have been in less exalted positions than mine. In fact I've pitied commoners who have married Crowned Heads. But it's happened to me and one can't argue with fate when it strikes so definitely.

Still, I did my stuff—I thought of him and told him so. I said it would be wrong for him to marry a girl like myself and that I wouldn't come between him and his mother or his people. He then proved that he really meant what he said. First of all he assured me I would not come between him and his people and that tne islanders would all love me, and were fond of the English. Then he intimated, though I think he sounded rather troubled about it, that his mother wanted him to be happy and would soon be won over. Mind you, I doubt that and I don't think he sees her with unprejudiced eyes as I do. The diplomatic world in general look on her as a—well I won't write the word. You know what I mean—she just IS one, and power-mad, too. I'm not surprised she wants him to marry the Duc d'Arlennes' daughter. She's very childish and would be a 'yes' girl for the Princesse.

Well, we argued for hours. I put up every obstacle I could think of in the way of our becoming even engaged, let alone married, but he talked me out of all of them. He said that I was the one who would make him completely happy and that whatever faults he had, or failings as a ruler, I had the intelligence and wit to be his finest friend and counsellor. Oh, and so many other things, Belinda. He went on and on. Finally he announced categorically that if I didn't marry him just because he was a Prince, he would renounce all his worldly goods and abdicate in favour of his cousin, and, come over and marry me just as Mr. Smith, Brown or Jones.

Darling Belinda, I can't tell you what I went through. Quite apart from his enormous attractions, I was so dumb-

founded and still am to think that I, little Catherine Leigh-Holmes, have awakened such a powerful emotion in a man like Dominic. Yet I can't deny what a strong magnetic force there is pulling us toward each other.

That particular morning (and I can hardly believe it was only a fortnight ago)—I was feeling a bit weak anyhow. Finally I gave in. I told Dominic that if he really felt it to be all right I would agree to an engagement. But it was not to be announced for another month at least, while he thought things over thoroughly and got the reactions of his Ministers and friends of the family, etc.

He spoke to Daddy. Daddy behaved like the real diplomat that he is. He told Dominic before we quit the Island that he was sure that I felt enormously honoured that the Prince of Montracine wanted me in marriage, but agreed with me that it was a serious step for him to take and that he must think well over it before announcing it to the world. Because, of course, of the vast difference in our positions.

Out came my darling Dominic with the names of all the Princes such as Rainier, who was a near neighbour of his own genre, and who had married a commoner, and how happy he was. Anyhow to please me and Daddy he finally agreed to wait for a month.

Two weeks of that have already gone and not an evening but he hasn't got on that private telephone line of his to London and spoken to me.

He refuses to discuss Montracinean affairs. He only hints that he has had some awkward moments with the Princesse and the Minister of State, and I don't doubt that little spy Leveuve has been getting at him in his slinky slimy way. But all he tells me is that he must see me soon and that if I don't marry him he will go crazy, I get letters too, Belinda. Wonderful, wonderful letters. Talk about romance, darling, I don't think it is given to many girls—particularly English ones – to be caught up in such a gorgeous glamorous whirlwind. I'm spinning around like a star in space, feeling weightless! I really am. I think poor Daddy's quite shaken because I go round with what he calls a long-distance look and forget everything! I used to scoff at romance, didn't I, Belinda? Now it's happened to me in such a terrific way, I won't ever be realistic or cynical again. Let those who scoff at romance do so. It does exist even in 1969 and is not just a thing out of a dead past.

Phone me as soon as you get home, Belinda, but if you don't intend to come soon, write and tell me if you think I'm stark staring mad to consider such a marriage. The trouble is that I don't think I can ever live apart from him . . ."

Mrs. Anders called up to Catherine, interrupting her thoughts.

"Can you come, please, miss?"

Catherine went downstairs.

"There's a trunk call for you. I answered it in Mr. Leigh-Holmes's study, miss."

Catherine knew who it was from even before she answered the call.

Her heart began to beat in that crazy way it always did when she heard the now quite familiar voice of Prince Dominic of Montracine.

"I'm ringing this morning because I want to warn you that you will be seeing me in six hours' time – that is, at five o'clock," he said clearly and with emphasis.

Catherine put a hand to one cheek and gasped:

"But *Dominic* —"

"Yes, I know you are going to tell me the month is not up," he interrupted, "but I cannot stand it any longer. These two weeks have been intolerable – besides it is a waste of time. I shall not change my mind and I pray you will not do so."

"I'll never change," she began, "but —"

"Then I am coming over," he said dramatically. "My pilot is standing by. I have some business to attend to but I shall leave here early this afternoon. I have already told Leveuve to make my reservations in London."

Catherine felt quite stupid. Her eyes had grown enormous.

"You shouldn't – oh, you should wait —" she began breathlessly.

"Are you giving me orders?" She heard the note of humour in his voice which she loved. If he had had no real humour she couldn't have agreed to marry him, for a shared sense of fun was an essential part of happy marriage. She recovered her equilibrium only sufficiently to ask whether he was bringing his secretary with him as usual. Dominic said no; he was coming alone, incognito, without even a detective.

"I shall be staying at the Connaught Hotel," he said. "I shall be known there as Monsieur Edouard. Edouard was my godfather's Christian name."

Catherine had a sudden desire to giggle.

"*Bonjour, Monsieur Edouard*," she said.

"*Bonjour, Mademoiselle Leigh-Holmes. Alors!*" he added on a caressing note that forbade further speech from her. "I shall be telephoning you as soon as I arrive. Keep this evening for me please, darling."

It was about half-past four when 'Monsieur Edouard' spoke to her again and this time his voice was so near – so near and so very dear. She gripped the telephone as though it were a talisman against all the sorrows of the world.

"You're here – in London."

"Yes, darling. Can I come and see you at once?"

No subtlety, no wasting time. She adored this side of her Prince. The very simple and forthright side.

"Yes. At once," she said breathlessly. "I'm quite alone. I'll fix dinner here if you'll have it with me. Daddy won't be back before eleven. Mrs. Anders is quite a good cook."

Then he laughed.

"That is superb. You for me to sit beside and a good cook to serve up our dinner."

"That sounds very French —" she began.

But he was speaking through the words.

"In one hour I will be there."

Heavens, she thought, *he comes at half-past five to dinner, my Prince.*

She called to Mrs. Anders who, apart from being a good cook, was an amiable woman and very fond of Catherine.

"I have a special boy-friend suddenly coming to dinner. What can you give us?"

"What would he like, miss?"

Catherine hesitated. Suddenly she realised that she didn't really know an awful lot about Dominic's personal tastes beyond the fact that he enjoyed English cuisine.

"No economy tonight, Mrs. Anders!" she sang out gaily. "Let's have your wonderful sole dish and then two marvellous English steaks."

"We-e-ell," came Mrs. Anders voice from the kitchen with faint protest. "Since when have I ever bought you 'orse-meat?"

"Okay," said Catherine, "and then some good strong Cheddar. He'll be tired of his creamy, runny French cheeses."

Mrs. Anders retired, and before sending Mr. Anders out with a shopping list, said:

"He must be very special – three courses. Soles is expensive and so is steaks, what with devaluation and all."

"Who's the bloke?" asked Mr. Anders, lighting his pipe.

"A Frenchy I should think – one of them diplomats."

"Miss Catherine is going it then while her Pa is out."

"Miss Catherine's a good girl and you hurry up, Alf Anders, or the shops will shut."

At half-past five precisely, 'Monsieur Edouard' presented himself at the little house in Chester Square.

Mrs. Anders had to answer the bell although Catherine had meant to do so but she was still in her bedroom. She was hurrying into a black and white spot voile-dress, sleeveless, frilled at the hem, and with a broad cherry-red velvet belt. It made her waist look extremely small. Eileen, the assistant who dressed her hair so beautifully, had pinned it all up on top this afternoon instead of letting it flow around her neck as usual. With her shining eyes and her face flushed from excitement, she looked charming and the first thing Dominic did was to tell her so.

He stood in the drawing-room looking out of the window when she came into the room. He swung round as he heard the door open.

"Charmante! Que tu es mignonne, Catherine!"

She looked at him with the same deep longing expressed in her own eyes. She admired his dark grey suit, his tie, the brown handsome glowing face.

"Oh, you do look so English suddenly!" she exclaimed.

"Good. I am English today – like the weather. It is raining," he said and laughed, and held out his arms.

They stayed for a moment in each other's arms, lips very close, then cheek to cheek. They were silent until suddenly Dominic gave a long sigh and said:

"I have wanted this, my Catherine, oh so much."

"Me, too," she whispered.

"Have you forgiven me for breaking our pact and not lasting out the whole month?"

"I'm glad. I think I'd have broken it if you hadn't."

"I love you so very much."

"And I love you. But oh, Dominic, is this wise?"

"Great love is often unwise. My love for you is so great that I can no longer sit down and analyse it coolly and try to decide – is *this* right? – is *that* right? – should I? – should I *not?* – oh, no, Catherine! What I feel in my heart for you will not allow me to be what you call 'wise', although I think I am now making the wisest choice of my life."

She dared not ask him what the choice was although she knew in her heart. She shut her eyes and pressed her face against his shoulder, still clinging to him. She felt his fingers caressing the back of her neck.

"Your hair looked so lovely. Now I have spoilt it."

"I couldn't care less."

"But I must still try to be wise enough not to compromise you. Shall we remain undisturbed?"

"Yes. Mrs. Anders will call us down to dinner at eight. The drinks are up here, and if the telephone rings I shall not answer."

It was his turn to close his eyes. He sighed.

"*Je t'adore!*"

It took a little more time before they could calm down and face realities. Then, with their drinks and cigarettes they sat together on the sofa; her hand locked in his, while he confessed what he had been doing in Montracine.

Last night he had told his mother that he intended with due formality, to ask Mr. Leigh-Holmes's permission to announce his engagement to Catherine.

She did not know whether to feel shocked, dismayed, or deliriously happy. She was speechless. Her fingers curled more feverishly around his hand and she shook her head from side to side as though she could not believe him.

It was crazy yet Dominic was far from crazy; she knew that. He was deadly serious. He had told his mother that if he could not marry Catherine, he would not marry anyone so there would be no direct heir to the Principality. She had warned him that there might be an uprising, especially in the Italian quarter, if he married Catherine. He had disagreed but had given her the alternative. She must conform and so must his Ministers, and acknowledge his marriage with what they called 'a commoner'. And after all Catherine was not really a 'Nobody'. Her father was in the Foreign Office. She came of an aristocratic English family. Whatever the Princesse said, Dominic knew that the Montracineans loved the English and welcomed tourists from the British Isles. And since his days at Oxford, Dominic had made excellent friends from England and the Commonwealth, and entertained them with his country's full approval.

"Whatever difficulties await me, I can overcome them. They cannot refuse to accept you and I am sure they will not wish to," Dominic assured her.

"But – Monsieur de Reynard —"

"Monsieur 'Fox' as you call him, my darling, will do as I command."

"He is such a powerful man and your mother likes him."

"My mother," said Dominic in a cold voice, "I both respect and admire and I have tried always to please her since my father died. But over my marriage I will not be dictated to either by her or anyone else."

"But oh, Dominic, am I – could I – are you *sure* I could fill such an important position as the wife of a ruling Prince in a Principality like yours?"

"You will fill it to perfection, Catherine. Quite apart from the fact that you were brought up in the diplomatic circle and are very far from being gauche and without knowledge of court etiquette, you are a very beautiful and distinguished girl. Nobody could criticise you."

"But they will —" she began with fear knocking at her heart.

"If the criticism is adverse, whoever makes it shall answer to me," he said vigorously.

It warmed her heart and restored the self-confidence that had been shaken by his astounding proposal. But still she found it hard to believe that he had gone so far as to announce to his confidential advisers, as well as his mother, that he intended to marry Catherine Leigh-Holmes.

"And you are quite sure that I could become – the wife of Prince Montracine – become a Princess – to your complete satisfaction?"

"Quite sure, Catherine. I have given it much thought – much, *much* thought, indeed."

"You do me great honour," she whispered.

"If you will agree to marry me, it will be you who will do me the honour," he said. Then he changed his tone and put an arm around her.

"My darling, you have gone quite white. Drink up your drink."

She gave a nervous laugh and shook her head.

"No, I'm all right. Just plain shattered. I knew that you had fallen in love with me, as I had with you but I did not think it would come to this."

He gave her a deep, all-embracing look.

"My darling love – there is no morganatic marriage in our country, and my great-grandfather who lost his wife when she was middle-aged never replaced her because he loved her so well. My grandfather also lived in great happiness with my grandmother until she died. And my father, although he was not a sentimental man, and more interested in politics and affairs of state than I am, deferred in all things personal to my mother. So you see, the Princes of Montracine have not made poor husbands, nor taken mistresses."

"If I thought marrying you would hurt you in any way, I think I'd even consent to be your mistress," she said recklessly.

He looked shocked.

"You must not say such a thing. It will anger me. I respect you, Catherine. I shall honour you always, no matter how old-fashioned that may sound in this day and age."

Tears which Catherine rarely shed suddenly sparkled in her eyes and on her lashes. She took his right hand and put it against her cheek.

"Oh, Dominic, Dominic, thank you. I love you very much," she whispered.

"Besides," he went on, "marriage with you could not possibly hurt me. You will see, my love, how gladly my people will receive you when I announce our engagement. You and your father shall fly over immediately and you shall be at my side when I speak to my people."

She made a last rather feeble effort to make him change his mind in case it should be right for him. Wildly thrilled, excited and flattered she might be, and she adored him, but even the thought of such a splendid marriage and life at his side on that glorious Island, in Le Petit Palais, could not blot out the memory of Princesse Isabella.

"Oh, Dominic, I'm afraid your mother doesn't like me."

"She will get used to the idea of our marriage. I think she does, in fact, admire you. It is only because she has some foolish wish to marry me off to the daughter of her great friend d'Arlennes that she has made a protest."

Catherine sat silent. She had an uncomfortable memory of the freezing expression on the face of the Princesse when she had walked into that bedroom in Le Petit Palais and found her son there.

But Catherine said no more because it was obvious that Dominic was going to argue her out of every protest she made. Besides it was, of course, what in her heart of hearts she wanted him to do. There was a snag in everything, she told herself, with a touch of cynicism; and the arrogant egotistical Isabella would make a formidable mother-in-law. That was certain. Dominic might get his own way but it would be she, Catherine, who would have to battle perpetually with that mother of his.

Yet helplessly, hopelessly in love as she was, she had to surrender because she knew that nothing now could stem the tide of his desire to marry her – nor alter her own wish to answer 'yes' to his proposal.

13

The most bitter day in the life of Isabella of Montracine was that on which her son – her only son and ruling Prince of the Island – was married with full pomp and ceremony to the English girl, Catherine Leigh-Holmes.

The wedding, which Dominic insisted should take place at once was solemnised in October, only four months after his engagement was announced.

The weather was poor. As so often happened on the Island, a sudden treacherous wind blew up on the wedding-eve, ruffling the calm blue waters of the Mediterranean. Montracineans awoke to a gale with angry seas lashing their coast and a remorseless downpour of rain. Inevitably it was cooler. It looked as though the brilliant summer had broken quite on the wrong day.

It had been arranged that Isabella should entertain some of the guests this evening, but in the midst of all the bowing and smiling, the flowers and champagne, the glitter and pomp of the royal wedding, Isabella had staged a sudden migraine. Making her apologies she retired and sent a message that she could not appear again that evening. The fact was that she could not bear further reminder of the bridal couple, of her son's triumph – his glowing face – and his bride's radiance.

So, thought Her Serene Highness, when she was alone in her room after the festivities had ended, her life, her heart were broken. Against all her entreaties and the advice of his Secretary of State and a number of close friends – he had passed by all the lovely aristocratic young girls with titles and wealth, and placed this little 'commoner' in *her* shoes. That was what bit like acid into the proud and egoistical heart of the Italian woman. She was in every respect now *the Dowager*. She would be shoved into the background in spite of Dominic's repeated vows that this would never be allowed. She had even moved from her apartment in the right wing of Le Petit Palais.

A month after the engagement there had been a scene with Dominic. He had begged her not to behave in a manner which more than suggested that she both disliked Catherine and disapproved of the marriage. She had absolutely no reason to feel such hostility towards Catherine. She was intelligent, but sweet and reserved, sometimes quite shy – why should she have to stand up to such undeserved antagonism? It distressed Dominic that she could not count on her future mother-in-law's affection. She had almost left him on one occasion. She and Isabella had clashed and Dominic sided with his future wife.

"I love her and I am going to marry her, and there is nothing that you can do about it," he had told his mother, "but please remember that it has never been my intention that you should leave the Palace, or create this atmosphere which can only have unhappy repercussions all round."

Nevertheless Isabella defied him. She was forced to put aside her personal feeling and attend the wedding, as she had attended the engagement celebrations, with a false sweetness which certainly had not deceived Catherine. It pleased Isabella that she had probably spoiled what should have been the girl's happiest day.

Now Isabella was installed in what she bitterly called 'the Dowager's House'; a large beautiful villa where her own mother had lived after she was widowed.

It was further down the mountainside enclosed in thickly wooded grounds. Isabella's staff went with her. Once there she made up her mind to attend none of the dinners or receptions that the young couple intended to give. She would plead ill-health and stay away.

But as she sat at her writing-desk this evening, looking at the proofs of the wedding photographs which had been taken and sent for her approval, Isabella's hatred of Catherine increased. Slowly but surely, it was developing into a dangerous obsession.

Strictly brought up in the Christian faith, she was half ashamed of her own jealousy but it had almost gone beyond control.

Her falcon eyes stared at one of the photographs. The best taken of the bridal couple, standing on the steps of the little Cathedral of Ste. Pierre, where, this morning, the wedding had taken place. Oh, it had been magnificent and attended by two Crowned Heads, innumerable lesser princes, and most of the relatives and friends with the exception of the Marquise de Courbese, Dominic's aunt, who had disapproved as much as his mother of the alliance. And of course, Isabella's sister, Térèsa.

Otherwise it had been a triumph for Dominic and even the unhappy Isabella had to admit that things had not turned out altogether as she had prophesied. There had been only a few murmurings in high places when the news first filled all the papers and journals throughout the globe. A few broken friendships such as that between Isabella and the old Princesse de Palvarias. The old lady, despite her infirmities, flew to the Island for the wedding – delighted that she had been the one to introduce the young lovers. Catherine Leigh-Holmes had certainly succeeded beyond Thérèse's wildest dreams and captured one of the most eligible young men in Europe. But because of the part the old Princesse had played in introducing them, Isabella barely spoke to her beyond the limits of courtesy.

Of course, Leveuve and de Reynard and their cronies gathered around Isabella expressing their shocked indignation, but 'the Fox' had at least consoled the Princesse by one sinister remark.

"All is not ended, Your Serene Highness. Is there not an English proverb: *'Marry in haste repent in leisure'?* I fear His Serene Highness has made too sudden a choice. Such a marriage *can* prove a failure, you know."

Alone this evening in her villa, Isabella went on staring at the picture of Dominic and Catherine standing on the Cathedral steps. The high wind had calmed down a little during the marriage service. The rain had stopped, but there was still no sunlight. Dark clouds had raced across a gloomy sky. Isabella experienced a petty satisfaction which she knew was unworthy because the bride had had to deal with such a tempest. Again and again her two pages had had to rearrange her billowing veil but there they stood – oh, how handsome Dominic was in his white uniform, his breast glittering with decorations. He was wearing full military dress, his sword at his side. And the girl – through slitted eyes Isabella looked at Catherine. Who could deny that she made a very beautiful bride? Hair perfect under a Limerick lace veil that had been her mother's, she was dressed with immaculate taste in ivory satin with long tight sleeves. Three rows of valuable pearls hung around her neck. Her mother-in-law had had to give her those. With great reluctance – but it had to be done, for the sake of appearances. But Isabella had felt as though a dagger had gone through her heart as she watched her son slip the gold circlet on to the bride's finger, and worse later, when Catherine knelt before her Prince and husband, and he gently placed a diamond circlet on her brow.

I shall never forgive him. I shall never like her. Isabella had thought and pretended to hide her bitter face in prayer.

Perhaps the most unhappy thing was her knowledge that Catherine had been such a success from the first day Dominic told his people he was going to marry Catherine Leigh-Holmes.

The Montracineans *liked* the lovely English girl. They liked a romance. This was truly romantic love. Aristocrats or peasants – all were satisfied by the knowledge that their young Prince had married a wife of his own choosing and looked so happy. And in everybody's mind there was the secret hope that next year perhaps, a son and heir would be born to Dominic IV of Montracine. *That,* Isabella thought, was a day she could hardly look forward to. How could she want a grandson with English blood in him and a mother who was just a little graduate from an English University. Isabella's Italian blood suddenly ran viciously hot. She took the photo-proof of the wedding couple between her thin jewelled fingers and tore it into tiny pieces.

The fishermen's boats in the harbour down at the Port rocked on troubled waters. It had started to rain again and the palm trees outside Isabella's villa waved violently in the wind.

But through it all Isabella could hear the sound of the music and dancing from thousands of homes on the island. The Montracineans continued to celebrate their Prince's wedding. They toasted Dominic, and his *Catrine* for that was what they called her, in French. *Princesse Catrine.*

The feasting continued all through the night. The Princesse had to ring for her maid and ask for a sleeping draught so that she could deafen herself to the unwelcome sound of rejoicing. Her common sense and the best side of her nature were drowned in the deep dark pool of her disappointment. Now and again she beat her clenched fists against her pillow and moaned aloud:

"Dominic, Dominic, my son, what have you done?"

When at the end of the Reception he had come with Catherine to say good-bye to his mother his dark bright eyes had beseeched her – silently asking for her co-operation and support.

Catherine seemed nervous but had been charmingly anxious to please, addressing her as Dominic had asked her to do by the name '*Maman*'. The very sound of that had made Isabella grit her teeth.

"As soon as we get back from the honeymoon we must have a little meal *à trois* and discuss the future," Dominic had said and kissed first his mother's hand, then both her cheeks. She had clung to him for a moment, her eyes full of tears more of anger than of sentiment, but Catherine she embraced coolly, barely touching the girl's forehead with her lips. So the couple had driven away to the airport, far too happy and oblivious of the bad weather to worry about *her* uncompromising attitude, Isabella was sure.

Late that afternoon her chagrin and misery were completed when Leveuve came to see her and bring a copy of the local evening paper.

"This will be figured in all the English, French and Italian papers tonight," he said.

She barely glanced at the photographs of the service in the Cathedral as well as the procession to Le Petit Palais for the Reception, although it brought back all the furious feelings that had possessed her when she saw, reproduced, her own glittering regal figure, wearing her tiara, standing beside Edward Leigh-Holmes. There were photographs of the whole wedding group; six bridesmaids including two English friends of Catherine's. The best man, Dominic's friend Patrick Guillemin; Sir Mark and Lady Daltry – all the relatives and close friends save Armand d'Arlennes and his daughter who had managed not to be present. They had gone to America on a visit and just not returned in time.

Another person to whom Isabella had taken a dislike was Marguerite Valencieux. As Dominic's godmother she had been sympathetic and charming about Catherine and told him that she saw no reason why he should not be immensely happy. Isabella felt betrayed by this.

In the secret place chosen by the young couple for their honeymoon, Dominic was, in truth, immensely happy and Catherine – hardly able to believe that she had exchanged the name Miss Leigh-Holmes for *Her Serene Highness Princesse Catrine*, could not have been happier. At the same time she was a little dazed. She felt as though she had been caught up in a veritable whirlwind of excitement, of splendour, and was still falling through space with only Dominic's strong arm to steady her.

They had mutually agreed to spend their two weeks together in the greatest possible seclusion. Dominic had accepted an offer from his first cousin, the Vicomte de Balençons to lend them the luxurious and secluded chalet which he owned high up in the French Alps. After the Palace it was perhaps small, even insignificant. But it had a certain beauty. It was panelled throughout in pine and furnished in modern Swedish style. Dominic had stayed there once before years ago, in the winter, joining his cousin for a ski-holiday, and liked it. It now seemed the perfect retreat for a *lune de miel*. There would be no reporters, no cameras, no prying eyes. Not a soul except the Balençons knew where the Royal couple were spending their honeymoon.

They travelled by air to the nearest town. There, Dominic drove a small hired car up the mountainside to the chalet which would be ever remembered by them both as heaven itself. Catherine was absolutely in accord with her husband. When he had asked her if she would prefer a more glittering holiday in the public eye – in America for instance, where they would be wildly welcomed – she had refused. She had had enough of being photographed and followed, even in London before the wedding. At first it had amused and thrilled her, then it became a bore, and often embarrassing. Daddy had threatened to leave Chester Square and hide somewhere until it was all over, but had stood by her nobly. It had all been rather like a bomb exploding at Catherine's feet once the papers announced the engagement. She could not get used to seeing her face beside Dominic's in every newspaper or journal she opened, on television, and the cinema news-reels.

Romance, ROMANCE ... the word was continually repeated. Handsome Prince Dominic of Montracine marrying the daughter of a London diplomat. Both so young and good-looking. Could it be more appealing to the human heart?

High up in these mountains on this night of nights, the weather was good at the end of a golden tranquil day. The autumn flowers were out in profusion, painting the countryside with vivid colour before the first snows should fall and bury them.

There were no formalities here. Dominic had absolutely forbidden it. Just one old serving man and a cook who had been in the Balençons family for many years. Neither of them had known who the bridal pair were until they arrived so could not be bribed to tip-off the Press. Not a soul in the village who saw them guessed at the identity of the young couple as they stepped out of the small car and walked hand in hand into the chalet.

When Dominic would have carried his bride across the threshold, Catherine laughingly protested.

"It's a gorgeous custom, but I'm much too heavy."

"Nonsense, you are as slender as a wand, my Catherine."

He carried her, stooping to kiss her rosy face.

Everything in the chalet seemed perfect. In the lounge, because the autumn was approaching and the night was a little cool, a huge pine log fire burned in the open grate. There were bearskins on the polished floor; a deep-cushioned sofa piled with pillows; soft lights, from brass hanging lamps, and books. And even a television which the couple swore, the moment they saw it, they would never turn on. They were going to do absolutely nothing this fortnight.

They were both fatigued. Catherine had never felt so tired in her life. She seemed to have been standing all day, and indeed for weeks past, what with fittings, photographs, and rounds of entertainment before she arrived on the Island.

Now it was *her* Island as well as his.

"Oh, Dominic," she said when they first walked into the chalet, "I want so much to be good for you – to love Montracine as much as you do – to make you proud of me."

"I have never been anything else," he said.

"Sometimes I'm afraid," she said. "The whole affair came so quickly – so unexpectedly. It has been such an upheaval in our lives. The other day I was just an ordinary English girl, and now I am the Princesse of Montracine. It staggers me."

"Do not think about that part, just remember that you are my wife," he said.

She could hardly forget it, she thought, looking at him with deep tenderness. He was so wonderful. Once she had imagined such a marriage impossible. There seemed so many obstacles. Dominic had overcome them.

She adored the chalet and particularly her bedroom. It was no bridal room of splendour and elegance such as would be waiting for them at Le Petit Palais. It was smaller and friendly, enchantingly simple. The four-poster bed had a conopy, and looped curtains of sprigged muslin, tied with white ribbons. The windows, shuttered at night, were framed in the same snowy frilled curtains.

On her dressing-table she found a huge bowl of white violets which had been flown from Montracine. With it, a note which said: '*From Dominic for My Wife and My Dearest Love for ever.*'

Close by, a mountain torrent gushed down into the valley. Catherine could hear the rushing sound of water, and the murmur of the green forest. Otherwise there was peace and silence.

But as she stood by the open window letting the mountain air fan her flushed face, a sudden feeling of terror seized her – a psychic terror that made her gasp. She remembered the words that the old Princesse de Palvarias had whispered as they kissed good-bye:

"I feel responsible for introducing you two wonderful people. I wish you happiness and a fine son for your Prince, my dear."

Supposing I never have a child, she thought, with that strange icy fear gripping her heart. Then she relaxed and laughed at herself.

She began to unpack. After her bath, she lay down for a moment on the big broad bed, closing her eyes. Really she was very tired. But through her mind there passed like a camera-film, the pictures of all that had taken place today. She could hear the rich thunder of the organ as she walked down the aisle with her bridegroom. He had taken her hand and pressed it because he saw her bouquet of lilies trembling. He was so dear, so kind and so simple, somehow, for all that he was Montracine's ruler.

She could have wanted the weather to be better. It seemed

awful to come to the Mediterranean and find storms instead of sunshine. But nobody seemed to care, and it wasn't at all like that day of Dominic's birthday, when nobody had really known who she was when she drove through the streets with him. The hundreds of Montracineans who lined the streets with waving flags and flowers today knew exactly who she was. They called out to her.

"Vive la Princesse Catrine!"

She had kissed her hand to them and that brought tumultuous applause. Dominic told her that already she had won their hearts because of her friendliness.

Then had come the Reception and the cutting of the huge bridal cake made by an amalgamation of Montracinean bakers; with white-iced gilded effigies of the Prince and Princess on the top of the towering four-tiered cake. Both of them had held on to Dominic's sword as they made the initial cut. Now Catherine could hear again the click of the cameras, the clapping of hands. She could feel her father's final embrace, and hear the words he whispered as he kissed her good-bye.

"It's been a great day for you, darling. I'm very proud of you. I like and respect my son-in-law. I only wish your mother had been alive to see it all."

Catherine wished it, too. She would certainly not find a new mother in Isabella.

The splendid wedding had been so feverish and crammed with incident that she could hardly remember anything after the ceremony but the sight of the dear old nurse, Augusta, standing in the row of servants waiting to congratulate their new Princess once they were back at Le Petit Palais.

Augusta's face was beaming:

"God Bless Your Serenity," she mumbled and thrust into Catherine's hand a parcel. The White Monkey, of course, wrapped in gold paper and tied up with ribbon. Catherine's favourite wedding present; and there had been such hundreds of them. Magnificent gifts from Crowned Heads, from friends and well-wishers all over the world.

The door gently opened. Dominic came in and walked to her side. He was already changed. They had both agreed that they should not dress up tonight, so he was wearing only dark blue slacks and a silky white polo-necked sweater. He looked down at her as though at something extremely rare and precious that overawed him.

"Catherine," he said, using the English name that he preferred. "Is it really you lying there? Are you really and truly my wife?"

She put up her arms and drew him down to her.

With his lips moving over her face, he murmured with almost desperate passion:

"You are – yes, you are, my very beloved wife."

Later he lay with his arm still around her and with his warm brown face against her neck and his fingers threading through her hair with inexpressible tenderness.

Nothing, she said to herself, *can ever be more wonderful than this and nobody can ever separate us, and I shall never be anything but the happiest woman in the world.*

Yet for the second time she felt baffled by a strange misgiving – a coldness that chilled her through from head to foot.

Should she even think such things? Was it tempting the gods? But as his lips touched hers again, all the warmth and ecstasy returned and she forgot everything but the tremendous happiness of this hour, this day, this night.

14

Of course, an enterprising young French reporter eventually discovered the honeymoon retreat of the Prince and Princess of Montracine. Within forty-eight hours there were headlines and photographs in the Press all over the world:

DOMINIC IV OF MONTRACINE WITH HIS BEAUTIFUL ENGLISH WIFE, CATHERINE. THE ISLANDERS CALL HER CATRINE.
(The young Prince and Princess arm-in-arm outside the door of the chalet smiling at each other.)

DAUGHTER OF ENGLISH DIPLOMAT, CATHERINE LEIGH-HOLMES, NOW HER SERENE HIGHNESS PRINCESS CATRINE, WITH HER ROYAL BRIDEGROOM.
(Delightful picture of husband and wife driving through the village being pelted with flowers by the children.)

And many other similar reports.

If it irked both Catherine and Dominic a little to have been discovered and followed, they were really too happy to mind very much.

For Dominic it was a revelation to be so free and so blissfully happy, even for a short time. For Catherine—it was unforgettable joy. Whatever faced them in the future, this honeymoon was the perfection of shared love, of mutual passion, with all the glamour and thrill which must necessarily surround the wife of a reigning Prince.

On the last night of their honeymoon they ate their evening meal, alone as usual, in the charming Swedish lounge – waiting on each other. Soft candlelight made a pool of gold on the polished table and there were candelabra alight on the high mantelpiece. Because the autumn night had grown a little cooler, the old serving man had lit an extra large fire. Fragrant, crackling, the pine-logs filled the room with warmth.

Catherine looked around and sighed. The chalet had grown so precious – so familiar. And there, opposite her sat her Prince in slacks and a jersey. She was similarly dressed. They might have been Mr. and Mrs. Smith – just *anybody*, she thought happily.

"Oh, Dominic," she said, "let's try to be like this sometimes even when we get back to Le Petit Palais. Don't let's have servants all the time while we eat. Let me look after you like an ordinary wife when we *aren't* entertaining."

"*When*," he echoed significantly, and laughed as he got up and lit one of the cigars he favoured. "But I am afraid you will have to do a lot too much of it for and with me, dearest."

"I know, and the Princess will have to be very correct and never let her Prince down, won't she?"

"My Princess is not capable of letting me down."

She put an arm through his and leaned her cheek against his shoulder.

"Don't love me too much, Dominic. I know that I feel the same way about you but sometimes I feel terrified . . ."

"Of what?"

She refused to tell him about that ghastly moment when she had wondered whether she would ever give him the heir he must have for his Principality. She moved away from him and put a disc on the record-player which their host had left for them. A French song she especially liked.

"*Je reviens te chercher.*"

"*I shall come back to look for you – to fetch you,*" she translated. "Would you come and look for me if I ran away?"

He blew a ring of cigar smoke towards her.

"Just try. I will use the *droit de seigneur*, quite apart from its usual meaning, and ring the Island round with gun-boats so that you could never get away from Montracine. So do not try."

"Don't challenge me," she laughed. "Remember my bulldog breed."

"I am not likely to forget it, sweet Catherine. During our two weeks here I have been bullied as never before in my life."

"How?" she demanded indignantly.

"For instance, insisting that I come with you for a walk – or go out to play tennis – or make love to you and kiss your eyes as well as your lips – or —"

"Now, Dominic," she interrupted warningly. "Be careful!"

He laughed and held out his arms. They were young, foolish, flippant and terribly in love.

That night, listening to her favourite waterfall and the piercing sweetness of a night-bird calling, Catherine wished yet again that they never need leave this mountain retreat. It was so like a stronghold against all the world's worries – against people like Isabella and de Reynard, and Leveuve. Ugh! she thought, remembering the veiled hostility in Leveuve's pale eyes when he had congratulated her after the wedding. How that man hated her! She would have many friends, but enemies, too; that was the fate of royalty.

She tried not to think too much about the future and

her fears. She concentrated on all those little domestic details which had delighted her here. She knew so much more about her Prince now in all such small unimportant yet essential ways. How much he preferred good crisp bread to the pastry flake of *croissants*; how little starch he liked in his collars; how little, really, he ate for one who must so frequently preside at banquets. The sort of after-shave lotion he used. The way he often shook back that dark lock of hair that would fall across his forehead. How he flung back his head and laughed like a boy at her jokes – and teased her in return. How he enjoyed reading to her – in French or English – the poetry he loved.

In their moonlit bedroom, Catherine lay thinking – thinking – unable to sleep, although he, her heart's desire, slept quietly beside her.

She put an arm across him and shut her eyes tight.

She prayed aloud as she had never done in her life before.

"Let me be good for him. Let me give him a son. Dear God, let us always be as happy as we are tonight."

15

One brilliant Mediterranean morning about three years later, letters from England were brought by the second post to Her Serene Highness, Princess Catrine.

At this time she was usually busy with her personal secretary, going through the appointments diaries, dealing with the charities, bazaars and hospital fêtes which she had to open, or answering her private letters.

Marie-Claire, the secretary, was young and charming. She was not a Montracinean but from Cannes, a first-class linguist and a sympathetic type of girl. Catherine liked her. She had two secretaries. The younger worked in an adjoining room and did most of the typing and filing.

During the three years that Catherine had been married to Dominic she had discovered that there was plenty for the wife of a Prince to do – quite apart from the domestic side. She had also found that it was difficult, if not impossible, to be an 'ordinary wife'. A housekeeper coped with the burden of staff problems and menus. The flowers were changed and arranged daily throughout the palace by local florists.

At times Catherine found hers an exacting position – more especially because so much had to be done without Dominic. Only when the day was ended could he remain with her. Only on the odd evening were they ever alone. Entertaining on a large scale went on daily. As did the necessity for Catherine to smile, to wave, to be well-dressed, always at her best in the public eye. In fact, she found it hard work to live up to her own ideals of how a Prince's wife should conduct herself.

The fact that Dominic's mother had retired to her villa and was no longer perpetually at her son's side, was some compensation. But Catherine felt strongly that Isabella had by no means given up her desire to influence Dominic, and have a finger in every political pie. More than once Catherine was made to feel the claw behind the velvet glove. On the surface, Isabella was less bitter and hostile than she had seemed at the beginning. But she still resented the marriage: Catherine knew that. On numerous occasions she was openly critical of Catherine; lost no opportunity to imply that she had had neither the upbringing nor training to grace her present position. When the Dowager Princesse was alone with Catherine, she would sometimes insinuate that the young couple were living in a world of dreams which was harmful to Dominic. He should, Isabella said, be regarded by the Montracineans and the outside world as a serious man, whose thoughts were more on the welfare of his Island than the romance of his marriage.

At first this spiteful attitude had little effect on Catherine. She used her intelligence and humour in order to ignore what she felt to be only the vapours of a jealous and disappointed woman.

But as the years went by, like the drop of water on the stone, Catherine's patience was worn down. Out of loyalty and consideration for Dominic's feelings, and because he was still devoted to his mother, she never repeated the things the Princesse said to upset her. But there were times when even she began to wonder whether or not they were justified. It was true that she, Catherine, and Dominic were still passionately in love and lived chiefly for the moments when they could be together. Time and custom had certainly not lessened his deep passion for her and she adored him. She could not have asked for a more devoted and charming husband.

But there was a new, disturbing unrest on the Island, creeping across it like a miasma. M. de Reynard was full of gloom about the attitude of the workers, particularly in the Italian zone, and Leveuve was these days always at Dominic's elbow, which worried Catherine. She believed him to be a hypocrite, and in a cold, calculating way he stirred up trouble in Dominic's mind.

Dominic laughed at Catherine's apprehensions, but even he could not go on being proof against the frequent gossip and internal strife among the Island labourers.

It was nearly two years before Catherine really understood what was going on behind Dominic's back.

She had learned that in such a position as hers she must never betray fatigue or fear. She must wear a mask. And so much a habit did it become that she began to wear one sometimes even when she was alone with Dominic. He seemed to be growing silent and depressed. Smothering her secret anxiety, she tried to be gay and warm and affectionate when she was with him, and to reassure him of her own content.

The sudden death of her father, at the end of the second year of her marriage, saddened her deeply. She had loved him with all her heart.

Now she felt she was all alone except for her husband, and she had no home other than Le Petit Palais.

She would never forget how good Dominic was to her at that time. He flew to England with her for the funeral and would not leave her alone for a moment. He was especially tender and considerate when they returned to Montracine. He begged her to ask some of her best-liked relatives and friends to stay at the Palace and said she must never lose touch with the England she loved, and which he loved, too.

Now she felt she was truly a Montracinean. She could even speak and understand the patois. She had made many friends on the Island both rich and poor. She experienced coolness only from a few of the close associates of her mother-in-law – her implacable enemy.

This morning, Marie-Claire, sorting through the post, handed the Princess the one letter she had been waiting for so anxiously during the last fortnight.

It was from a London gynaecologist whom she had visited when she flew over to London on an unofficial visit at the beginning of the month.

She had stayed in the Clinic for several days having exhaustive tests. The results, she gathered from this report, were satisfactory; there seemed no reason why she should not have a child. *But the fact remained: she had been married for three years and had not conceived. And there was nothing further this specialist could do.* Even Dominic, himself, had consented to have tests, in Paris. There seemed no reason why he should not father a son.

But we just don't manage it, Catherine thought miserably.

And now her last hope seemed to have gone.

Suddenly, unable to bear Marie-Claire's furtive but sympathetic gaze, she folded the letter and walked quickly out of the room. She locked herself in her bedroom, lay down on her bed, pressing her face to the pillow, choking with sobs.

There was nothing to be done but go on hoping the letter said. And that was what they all said.

Nothing seemed wrong, yet there was nothing to be done.

At the end of the first year Catherine had been only slightly disappointed and troubled because she did not become pregnant. But at the end of eighteen months, she had started the dreary, soul-destroying round of doctors and professors which gradually undermined her self-confidence that she would ever conceive.

Time and time again she had hoped . . . tried to believe that there was no reason that the great event would not take place very soon. Time and time again she had been doomed to disappointment.

After the second year she began to feel desperately anxious. Now she knew that her fears were shared by Dominic.

She knew, too, that this was a yardstick that could be used against her by her mother-in-law. An accusation against which she had no defence.

She was letting her husband down. She was letting down his country. Not once but a hundred times her mother-in-law reminded her that one of the chief reasons the Montracineans had wanted their Prince to marry was the vital need for an heir. The matter had even crept into the Press. Catherine was ashamed of seeing her most private affairs in cold print in foreign newspapers, although Dominic was marvellous and repeatedly told her that it didn't matter. Nothing mattered but that they loved each other. But she could not bear those cuttings – cruelly pointed out to her by Isabella.

The world pitied her. Catherine was raw with wounded pride, with sorrow for Dominic much more than for herself.

UNHAPPY PRINCESS SEEKS ADVICE FROM YET ANOTHER SOURCE.

STILL NO SIGNS OF AN HEIR FOR MONTRACINE. GROWING DISSATISFACTION THAT THE ENGLISH PRINCESS HAS NOT GIVEN HER HUSBAND A SON.

(Etc. etc.)

Catherine began to sense a mixture of pity and coolness in the glances thrown at her in public on the Island. There were relatives such as Dominic's aunt, his godmother, and one or two others on the Italian side who mentioned when they met her that it seemed 'so sad' they had no child. She began to feel hunted. Even the staff watched and waited and whispered among themselves; she was sure.

Then there was the constant humiliation and physical misery of the numerous examinations – doctor after doctor, clinic after clinic – useless treatment. Dominic would have spared her these things but she insisted on trying everything. She now envied the lowest and poorest of the women islanders who seemed able to produce a baby with the greatest of ease.

No money had been spared. The Princess was visited by professors from Vienna, from Berlin, from a great Russian specialist working in Paris, even from America. They all tried to help – to say there was still plenty of time. But they could do nothing. There seemed nothing to do. They all begged her to keep calm and stressed the point that emotional tensions were bad for her.

She took endless pills; went through endless treatments, all of which had no effect except to exhaust her and cause her fresh distress. A distress that was heightened because Dominic felt it, too. Often they expressed their despair together. But he would never let those moments last. He was quick to take her in his arms and show that he was still the adoring lover, and that he believed that one day the wanted child would appear.

After another year of frantic futile effort Catherine felt stunned. Her whole personality was beginning to change. A lot of her old humour had gone, and her former complacency. Even her intellect seemed drained; she no longer wanted to read or to learn. She was beginning to feel ill and to develop an inferiority complex. Every time a child was born to some well-known person on the island and the bells rang for the Christening, the sound seemed to eat into her soul—destroy her afresh.

She had been so hopeful about this, the latest London specialist to treat her—and who was supposed to have found new methods of ensuring pregnancy.

The poor report that arrived on this bright beautiful morning was a mortal blow to Catherine. She felt she could hardly bear to show the letter to Dominic.

Somehow she must pull herself together, dry her tears and make herself look attractive. After lunch she was opening a new wing in the local Home for Spastic Children. She must get herself into the frame of mind to chat happily with the Matron and nurses and talk brightly to those poor little children.

Oh God, she thought, *why did this have to happen to me? Why am I barren? Why?*

Somehow it had never entered her mind that she might fail to give birth to a child. Only up at the chalet on her honeymoon, the icy hand of doubt had touched her—but she had been happy and confident then and dismissed her fears.

She wrote often to her best loved cousin, Belinda.

Belinda was a realist. The last letter she had sent to Catherine a week ago had been full of sympathy about this continued infertility but gave Catherine some pretty pungent advice.

"*When I saw you the other day I thought you looked thin and a bit haggard, my sweet. Take your cousin's advice and don't let yourself go just because you're finding it difficult to have a baby. You don't want to lose your looks at your age and you will if you mope around. Dominic won't like it."*

'*Mope around!*' Is that what she was doing these days? Catherine asked herself. She tried so hard not to let anybody see how she fretted.

But of course she knew that the whole thing was beginning to get her down. The watching, the waiting, the hoping, then the crashing down into the dark despair again. Certainly she didn't want to lose her looks for darling Dominic's sake. She would have to make just a bigger effort to conceal her feelings.

She smoothed over the bed which she had rumpled. Her fingers came in contact with the White Monkey. The old toy usually sat there on her pillow. She looked at the wizened amusing face sadly.

"What's happened to you, my mascot? Why don't *you* do something for me?" she asked with a wry smile.

A knock came at the door. She unlocked it. Her mother-in-law's Italian maid was standing outside. The woman curtsied and told her that Her Serene Highness wished to see the Princess Catrine if she would please go over to the villa. Isabella had arranged to lunch with Catherine but was just recovering from a migraine and would rather not move from her chaise-longue. The Princess Catrine would find her on the terrace.

Isabella was the last person Catherine wanted to see in her present unhappy mood, but she told the woman she would go to her straight away.

Isabella lay on the terrace of her palatial villa, a sombre figure as usual in black. She was wearing dark glasses and suddenly Catherine was struck by the fact that her face was thinner than it used to be. She was gaunt, older, and certainly losing *her* looks. She used to be so handsome, even charming when she wished. But the charm, too, had gone. Catherine now knew that she must expect an unpleasant interview. The woman was spiteful and jealous. Catherine could almost pity her. She was taxing Dominic's affection if she only realised it.

"I'm sorry you are ill, Maman"–Catherine began. The name 'mother' always seemed to stick in her throat. Never at any time had Isabella attempted to be a mother to her son's wife.

"Thank you," said Isabella with her customary chilliness of voice and manner, but ever polite. "Sit down, Catrine. I wish to talk to you."

She spoke in her own language. She seemed to take an acid pleasure in straining Catherine's knowledge of Italian to its uttermost.

Obediently Catherine seated herself in the basket-chair with its dark blue cushions, beside the chaise-longue. A manservant brought out a tray with iced lemonade. It was a hot morning. The Princesse removed her dark glasses, and Catherine saw the black piercing eyes running over her critically.

"Your dress is a little too short. It is not dignified," said the older woman.

Catherine had forgotten that she had put on this pink 'cotton' which although not in any way a 'mini', was shorter perhaps than the dresses worn by most of the women surrounding Isabella.

"I won't wear it again, Maman," she said.

Isabella went on staring at her daughter-in-law. There was a moment of silence. Catherine had grown used to these silences between them. She felt that Isabella was well aware that they had an unnerving effect. If she had something disagreeable to say, why didn't she get it out, and be done with it?

The Princesse's next words were more than disagreeable, they were blunt – less coated with the kind of sugar that sickened Catherine because she knew the bitter taste of the medicine to come.

"It is time, Catrine, that you realised how displeased I am. We must talk seriously about the future."

"Whose future, Maman?"

Isabella waved a hand.

"Primarily Dominic's and, of course yours. Mine also because I am deeply concerned."

"I don't think I understand —" began Catherine.

"I am speaking mainly," broke in Isabella, "of the future of our country and of our people."

For a moment Catherine was puzzled and not very alarmed.

"Is anything wrong? Has something happened in our country that I don't know about, Maman?"

Isabella's thin lips twisted into a caustic smile.

"There is a lot you do not know about, *mia figlia*. You may think you have knowledge of the people here but I assure you even after three years, you are still virtually a stranger."

Catherine flushed.

"You think the islanders regard me as a stranger? I didn't imagine so. They always receive me so well."

Isabella shrugged.

"Oh, the crowds are sheep. One waves and cheers, the rest follow. And for Dominic's sake they make a show of welcome for you."

"I see. The cheering is not really for me."

Like a cruel arrow Isabella's swift reply went through her heart.

"And it never will be while you remain childless."

Catherine gasped. She clenched both her hands until the

knuckles gleamed white. She felt sick. She wanted to choke, to get up and run away – run as far away as possible from this ruthless, malicious woman who had *never* welcomed her, never wanted her for a daughter-in-law and never stopped making her feel awkward.

She had often accepted Isabella's cruelty for the sake of the husband she adored, or they would have quarrelled openly long ago. But this was the unkindest cut of all. She was about to express her indignation when she remembered an incident of her childhood. A little friend had upset her and she had turned on the other child, and talked to her spitefully. Afterwards, her father who had been present, said to Catherine:

"My very dear little girl, it is in the nature of man to turn and try to hurt the person who has hurt him. But such a policy does more harm than good. It doesn't even cancel out the original injury. It swells the animosity between the two people concerned. Politicians and diplomats have to learn to accept open jibes and insults. Nothing can be more galling to the enemy than if one puts up a smiling front and pretends one has not even felt a scratch. Try to remember that."

She did remember it – now. Darling Daddy! He had been proved right so often in the things he had taught her.

She got her feelings under control and spoke quietly to the woman lying on the chaise-longue.

"I am quite sure that my not having a baby – not giving Dominic an heir – is the source of immense disappointment to everybody. Mainly to Dominic, and naturally to you, too, Maman. I've tried everything – you know that. I've had to go through some pretty humiliating and unattractive examinations. It hasn't been easy for me."

The Princesse's gaze continued to be antipathetic.

"I do not for one moment suggest that it is your fault,

Catrine. I have even admired the way you have made these efforts. But the result is the same. You do not seem able to bear a child and Montracine deplores this. There is growing dissatisfaction on the Island. You know quite well that a man like Dominic who controls an important Principality must have children. All of us have looked forward to the arrival of a son and heir; or failing that, even a daughter; someone at least to carry on the line."

Catherine went on clenching and unclenching her hands. Her nerves were none too good this morning and she was being driven into a corner.

"I know, Maman. Don't you suppose I am more disappointed and upset than anyone?" Her voice rose a little.

Isabella held up a hand.

"Quietly, please, Catrine, one does not wish your voice to be heard by the staff."

Catherine made no reply. She turned her head over her shoulder and stared blindly at the beautiful formal gardens of the villa. It was all so splendid. Up in Le Petit Palais it was even more splendid and beautiful, and however unkind Dominic's mother was to her, she, Catherine, remained Her Serene Highness, the First Lady of the Island. But, oh God, what did it matter? What was all the magnificence and glory worth if she was to be denied the joy that was every woman's rightful heritage—motherhood?

Isabella's icy voice continued.

"I sympathise with your personal feelings, but we who occupy positions such as yours and mine—who have become the wives of reigning Princes—cannot consider our personal feelings. We must be concerned only with the welfare of husband and State."

Catherine pushed a heavy wave of hair back from a forehead that was growing damp with perspiration. She wished her heart would not beat so fast and that she did not feel so hopelessly incapable of dealing with this grim woman.

Dominic did not really know his mother. To him she presented an affectionate, kindly side. He had often told Catherine that he was aware that Maman was difficult but that her 'bark was worse than her bite'. But Catherine knew full well that the newspapers at home and elsewhere in the past had not been wrong in summing up the Princesse's character. She was ambitious and ruthless. Her bite was every bit as bad as her bark, Catherine thought, and once more had to clench and unclench her fingers in order to keep her self-control. She could so easily have burst into tears and screamed at Isabella:

"*Stop nagging at me. Stop being so beastly. Stop making me feel that I am entirely to blame and should never have married Dominic.*"

On this brilliant beautiful morning, for the first time throughout the three wonderful years of sharing her life with him, Catherine suddenly went down to the depths and began to ask herself that very question.

Should she have married him? She had taken an awful gamble. Yet she had never felt until now that she had disgraced him or her important status throughout the years. Until she heard what Isabella had to say this morning, she had imagined herself in favour with the Montracineans whom she loved. She believed they thought well of her. But that wasn't what really mattered. It was this tragedy of being childless.

"What can I do about it, Maman?" Suddenly she lifted her head and looked with beseeching eyes at her mother-in-law. "What more can I do? Heaps of people tell me that as our tests—both Dominic's and mine—have shown no signs of—of inadequacy, I might still become pregnant at any time."

"But that time might well come too late," said Isabella with her freezing smile.

"Too late for what?"

"For Dominic's good. You do not realise it but he has quite often been severely criticised over his marriage. Until he met you, you must know the whole Island expected him to marry Sophie d'Arlennes."

Catherine's feelings got the better of her.

"Oh, yes. I know that! But Dominic loved me. And what right have you to suppose your precious Sophie wouldn't have failed him just as I seem to have done? Heaps of other women remain childless and through no fault of theirs. Just something to do with, just—oh, it is just *not right*!" she finished lamely.

Isabella reddened angrily.

"You are using an unfortunate tone to me, Catrine. And there is absolutely no reason why 'my precious Sophie' as you call her with such lack of courtesy, would have been barren like yourself."

Catherine sprang to her feet. This was too much. Not even the memory of her father's counsel could keep her calm.

"I'm *not* necessarily barren. No one has ever said so. None of the specialists I've been to."

"Indeed?" murmured Isabella looking up at the girl's flushed unhappy face without sympathy.

"None of them," said Catherine between her teeth.

"Then it seems very strange, Catrine, that no child has made an appearance. You were in London only a week or two ago, were you not? Has your new English specialist there given you hope?"

"No." The answer was forced from Catherine and tears glittered on her lashes.

Isabella gave an effective sigh.

"How very sad. Please do not think I have no pity for you. But I happen to be Dominic's mother and, as one time wife of the ruling Prince of this Island, I know what is best for our people. You are still young and inexperienced. I presume you think that it does not matter much whether you present Dominic with an heir or not."

Catherine gave her a wild look.

"Of course it matters but what can I *do?* It's a tragedy – for all of us – but even if I'm to blame – what can I do?"

The Princesse linked her long thin fingers together and gave another sigh.

"I see no reason to prolong this unhappy conversation. You have become hysterical. I dislike hysterical women. You must decide for yourself what you think you should do. I have no advice to offer. I merely repeat that I am concerned about my son and the feeling in Montracine. Now would you kindly ring for my maid. I wish to go in. It is too hot out here. I was improving an hour ago but my head has started to ache again and your attitude has not made it any better."

Catherine smothered a truly hysterical desire to laugh. *Her* attitude. Really, this woman was a monster. She knew full well what was at the back of that cunning mind. A solution that made Catherine's heart sink like a stone and her blood run cold. She would not voice it even to herself.

Before she could move, Henri Leveuve appeared through one of the open French windows. He looked slightly less smooth and unruffled than usual. He gave Catherine a quick look out of the corners of his eyes, then approached the older woman, bowing.

"Your Serene Highness's pardon. I have information that cannot wait."

He handed Isabella a folded note. She read it quickly and smothered an exclamation.

"Who is dealing with this, Henri?"

"Monsieur de Reynard and—" he reeled off several names of top-ranking officers in both the Army and the Police Force on the Island.

Isabella looked perturbed. She sat upright, fanning herself with a rapid movement.

"Keep me further informed, Henri. Where is His Highness?"

"Coming to see you, Madame. He has of course been exceptionally busy."

"I imagine so," said Isabella under her breath.

Leveuve gave Catherine another look, one of those rather veiled unpleasant looks which never failed to make her feel uneasy. She only knew that the man hated her and that through the three years of her marriage had shown an unrelenting animosity that almost matched Isabella's. But to Dominic he remained the efficient and apparently devoted secretary. The 'yes' man whom Catherine despised.

Alone once more with her mother-in-law, Catherine said:

"You have obviously had bad news, Maman. Shall I leave you?"

"No," said Isabella in a harsh voice. "You shall hear exactly what is going on."

A nervous tremor went through Catherine's whole body. She stood silent, waiting, positive now that the bad news in some way concerned her, and that Isabella was gloating over it.

"There have been factory strikes in the Italian zone," said Isabella fixing her daughter-in-law with her baleful gaze. "A march, headed by Luigi Moldini, an Italian, reached the Church Square in the Port an hour ago. There have been ugly scenes. The mounted police tried to keep order because there were windows broken and some fighting. During the scuffle, the child of one of the shopkeepers ran out and was trampled underfoot by a horse of the Household Cavalry, after which there was chaos, although it was purely accidental. No doubt you do not know, and I was not told until now, that Dominic has been down there in person for the last hour trying to restore order and confidence."

Catherine felt cold. She put a hand to her throat.

"My God . . . but what triggered this off? . . . what is it all about?"

"It is the first demonstration of the kind I can remember in my lifetime on our Island," continued the Princesse's chilling voice. "I am informed in this letter from the Chief of Police that the trouble has been brewing for a long time. Luigi Moldini is not only demanding higher wages but a change in the legislative power that rests now with my son and the National Council. The main cause of all the unrest was voiced aloud this morning—the fact that there is no heir. The Montracineans feel no security and say that their Prince is more interested in his childless English wife than his Island."

A feeling of nausea rose in Catherine. She looked wildly at her mother-in-law.

"But they l-love D-Dominic," she stammered, "they *l-love* him."

"They did," Isabella corrected, "and still would if things were different, but unless we are careful they will demand his abdication and the return to this Island of his cousin, Prince Louis, who already has a son and heir."

16

For over an hour Dominic and Catherine had been talking. It was the only occasion that they were alone together, that either of them could remember such precious moments being so spoiled, so unhappy.

Lunch was over; they sat on the covered terrace outside Dominic's private suite, finishing coffee. Dominic who so far had been walking up and down agitatedly smoking cigarette after cigarette, was persuaded at last to sit down quietly with his wife. When he looked at her it was with the utmost concern. Sun-tanned though she was, he could detect the underlying pallor. The fine green eyes, so famed for their beauty and brilliance, were reddened by weeping. She, too, was smoking, and he could see how her fingers shook as she lifted the cigarette to her lips. The atmosphere was still tense. The young Prince of Montracine had been brought face to face for the first time with the ugly truth.

This English girl whom he had made his wife and close companion and whom he adored, was as much the cause of this morning's rebellion as the workers' dissatisfaction. Not only her childlessness but his government were now being openly criticised by the Montracineans.

Again and again he said to Catherine:

"My private life is my own. I will not be told by the people what to do when it concerns my marriage – my wife."

Catherine, feeling as though every inch of her body had

been physically savaged as well as her consciousness, kept answering:

"It is me they really blame – not you, *me* – and you must accept the fact that your country – anybody's country – is virtually controlled by its inhabitants. Therefore, you have to do as you are told. Hasn't it been so throughout history? Look what happened to the King of France who refused to listen to adverse criticism of Marie-Antoinette."

To that, Dominic had argued:

"A ridiculous comparison. Marie-Antoinette was a foolish, ill-advised woman who behaved without heart to a starving nation. You have done everything on earth you could for my people."

"Everything but the one most important to them. I have not given Montracine an heir."

Again and again Dominic argued that it did not matter – that in spite of this tragedy he would rather have her with him than anybody else in the world. Childless or not, she was the one he loved. He would never change. That was the statement which made her cry so much, and why the practical, sensible Catherine had given place to a passionate, emotional woman still desperately in love with her husband. As many times as Dominic protested his love for her, she responded, assuring him of hers.

But nothing could alter the present situation. It made Catherine shudder even now to remember the scene that had evolved between Dominic, his mother and herself. Soon after Leveuve's visit, the Prince arrived at the villa, looking haggard and shaken, but trying to shrug the trouble off as being of no vital importance.

"We read every day of strikes and marches, all over the world. Why should not we put up with a taste of it on our own Island? Moldini has always been an insolent fellow and a troublemaker and, of course, it was sad and tragic that

that poor little child was involved. That was my main sorrow. I went to see the parents," he added sombrely.

"And I know what they said when they saw you," Isabella cut in.

"How do you know?" he had demanded.

"I was told. It is Catrine they blame!" she said furiously.

Then for the first time Dominic openly quarrelled with his mother, accusing her of gathering spies around her, and of interfering with his methods of government. Stung by this, furiously jealous of Catherine who was standing by in silence, the Princesse also lost her temper.

"The parents said openly that you could not know what it means to lose a child. They all think that you care more for your wife than your Principality. It was even shouted in the Square this morning that maybe the English girl did not wish to spoil her figure with a pregnancy."

That had shocked Catherine to the roots of her being and never would she have believed that her gentle Prince could turn with such rage and fury on his once-loved mother. Violently he disputed the disgraceful allegation. Catherine, he said, had done everything in her power to bear children. They had both done what they could. They had been denied the privilege of parenthood through no possible fault on either side. Furthermore, he accused Isabella of giving no affection and little help to her daughter-in-law.

At this point Catherine tried to intervene, even to defend her mother-in-law. She did not want to be the cause of a rift between mother and son – for Dominic's sake.

She forced out a denial:

"Maman has never hurt me. She has done her best to help me fulfil my obligations as your wife, Dominic. Please do not make things worse by blaming her. It is obviously all my fault."

When Dominic started to deny this fiercely, the Princesse

threw her son a reproachful look and walked away, refusing to return.

It seemed to Catherine now, as she stared across the familiar glorious panorama of mist-blue mountains and shimmering sea, that the beauty and the glamour were all ruined. Her marriage to Dominic had been a glorious personal success, but from his point of view as Ruler of the Principality, a total failure. It was a grim truth for her to swallow. She felt mortally hurt today, particularly by that jibe about her trying to prevent pregnancy. She could not bear it. It was too bitter to be endured.

Down below the balcony in the hot October sunshine, the vineyards were heavy with sweet grapes; the fields looked richly gold. The grain had been gathered in and stacked.

On the surface everything seemed as usual on the Island. But underneath there was a poison which had only just a few hours ago erupted like a volcano. A poison which Catherine felt sure had been created by the Princesse's sycophants, and the Palace spies who were in her pay.

Now, with everything drained from her face save grief, she stared at Dominic. He had aged, she thought miserably. Aged since she had seen him first thing this morning. Then, as usual, he had taken her in his arms and kissed her – like a lover. Three years of being her husband had not decreased his passion for her.

"Dear God – what are we going to do?" she whispered.

Dominic, his lips thinly repressed, jabbed a cigarette-end into an ashtray.

"*You* can do nothing, my Catherine. You have done enough for the ungrateful people. But I want you to cancel any public appearances you may have arranged for the next few days. What have you on?"

"I was visiting the Home for Spastic Children and having

tea with the Matron later today. In fact I ought to go and change and get ready now."

"No—please ask Marie-Claire to telephone and say you cannot attend, say you have a temperature—anything you like."

Catherine flushed.

"No, darling, I must go, just as though nothing is wrong. I am not going to be frightened off. I am your wife and it would be a show of weakness or fear if I cancelled my engagements."

He protested. She argued. Then he gave up. He knew the strength of his Catherine's character. He could not admire her more. His bitterness against the uprising which had involved her integrity stabbed him to the heart. He leaned forward, took her right hand and kissed it.

"Do as you like, my Catherine. I think as a matter of fact that I am unnecessarily alarmed. Moldini's little affair can in no way emanate solely from this question of an heir. They are making that an issue, but what they want is more money, like all these workers today. I have called a special meeting of the Council. All members are assembling at five o'clock. We must of course, deal with Moldini and the position of the strike—before other matters."

"Things on this Island have changed since I first came, Dominic," she said sadly. "If you will forgive me saying so, it was your mother then who was not very popular. Now it is I."

Dominic got up and Catherine, looking up at him, read a new strength and hardness on that handsome young face. But hostile though she was to Isabella, it distressed her to hear him declare that he did not wish to discuss his mother. It made her feel so guilty—innocent though she was.

Dominic said:

"Anybody who hurts you, hurts me. I will not tolerate

villainous criticism of you. I shall find out who is mainly responsible for it. And I shall put an end to spying within the Palace. You told me, didn't you, that the news about this morning's affair was taken to my mother by Leveuve?"

"Yes."

Dominic's eyes narrowed.

"I gave no orders that any such note should be delivered. On the contrary, I wished the information to be kept from both you and my mother until I, myself, came back."

Now for the first time in the three years of her marriage, Catherine stated frankly what she really felt about his private secretary.

"He is always going behind your back to Maman. He hates me and I wouldn't wonder if he doesn't send secret information to your cousin, Prince Louis, as well as Maman here."

Dominic stood still, staring at his young wife.

"You think Leveuve has been plotting with somebody in a higher position to bring Louis back here?"

"I don't go as far as that, but I know he is not loyal to you, Dominic. *I know it.*"

"If I thought —" began Dominic under his breath, but Catherine interrupted.

"For God's sake, Dominic darling, don't be in a hurry to do anything, no matter what we both imagine. Let everything simmer down. This would not be the right time to dismiss any of your immediate staff, and start fresh trouble. But I would like to see the day when neither de Reynard, nor Leveuve is near to you. I distrust them both. But I shall never be like your mother – I shall never try to take an active part in governing. That is why I have said nothing about Henri until today."

"You are very loyal and very lovely," Dominic said. And for a moment the cares and worries seemed to fall away from his face like a mask. He looked young and tender again. Leading her into the cool beautiful room where they had spent so many happy hours together with their music, their books, their private dinner-parties, he took her in his arms and held her close.

"I love you so very much. You are right when you tell me to take no drastic action, my wise Catherine. But I shall watch Leveuve from now onwards and remember your warnings."

"I may be wise but I am pretty hopeless about having that baby, aren't I?" she said with a laugh that verged on tears.

"I refuse to let this thing become a knife that they can plunge into your heart," he said with drama. "I refuse to let you feel guilty. There can be no guilt attached to childlessness."

"But perhaps if you were married to someone else —" she began, only to be interrupted once more and this time with a force that could leave no doubt in any woman's heart that she was beloved.

"I refuse to listen to such a thing. Never let me hear you say it again. You are my wife, my darling, and you will be my wife until the end."

She clung to him, weeping now.

"But Dominic, Dominic, suppose the years go by and I never have an heir. You can see what is brewing up among the Montracineans. It's no longer a secret."

"Nevertheless, heir or no heir, I shall never let you go," he said. "*Never.*"

After he had left her for the conference in the Assembly Hall, Catherine changed into one of her most attractive white ensembles, and put a big white hat on her head, and drove down to the Home for Spastic Children.

Marie-Claire leaned forward and showed her a packet of letters in envelopes of varying shapes and sizes.

"You will not want to see these, I am sure, Madame. They are all advertisements – the usual."

Catherine waved them aside. Yes, she knew only too well about such things. Everybody in Europe – farther afield than that, for it had appeared also in the American Press – knew that she had no child. Streams of letters reached her regularly from every kind of quack or clinic – from religious organisations, spiritualists, herbalists. A fantastic variety of sources. Some pamphlets she kept, hopelessly. Most of them she threw away. She rarely showed any of them to Dominic. But at times, Catherine even while she lay in her husband's arms, asked herself:

"*Would it have been better if we'd never met? I've failed the one human being in the world I'd gladly die for.*"

The fact that he was so patient, so sweet about her childlessness, so immensely kind always, seemed to make things worse.

Sighing deeply she picked up a letter marked '*Confidential*' and bearing a Geneva postmark.

Interest and warmth suddenly returned to her face as she looked at this letter, written by a Swiss-French physician, one whose name she had heard, but had not so far consulted.

She read what he had to say from start to finish, read it two or three times, then stood up.

Her secretary, glancing at the Princess, noted that her cheeks suddenly held more colour. She looked brighter.

"Marie-Clare," she said, "this is in strict confidence. I want you to get this telephone number – it is a Clinic on the outskirts of Geneva. Ask to speak on my behalf to Professor Chambertin. Arrange for him to fly over and see me here as soon as possible. All his expenses will, of course, be paid."

"*Oui*, Madame," said Marie-Claire, and sat down at her desk and lifted the telephone receiver as her illustrious employer walked out.

Marie-Claire adored the Princess Catrine. She had at first thought she might not care for the Prince's English-born wife, but she was now one of her most devoted admirers. She had never known anybody more thoughtful or generous, and there were times when they walked and laughed together like friends. There was no snobbery about Princess Catrine.

Everybody knew, of course, of her tragedy . . . her incessant search for some kind of help which would give her her heart's desire. It had infuriated Marie-Claire whenever she heard the English girl criticised harshly.

Marie-Claire knew well – perhaps a little more than the Princess – about the vital necessity for an heir. If anything happened to the Prince, Catherine still in her twenties, would never be allowed to govern, neither would the Island wish Isabella to take the reins of full power between her hands. They would sooner that Prince Louis returned to Montracine. At least he had already a ten-year-old son, and two small daughters.

As for Moldini and the unrest that was seeping from his crowd into the rest of the Island, Marie-Claire knew all about that, too. Her father had business interests in the factory at La Cina. He had been saying only last night that Moldini was a powerful enemy and had already a big following. He had done a great deal of harm. Marie-Claire's father complained that men were like sheep who followed blindly, and that the Montracineans on the French side of the Island might soon be dangerously influenced by Moldini against the present régime. Nothing would turn the tide against the young Prince if he remained childless. Then Marie-Claire had exclaimed that the Princess was a lovely and noble person, and she and the Prince loved each other devotedly. They should not be made to feel responsible for something that was out of their control.

"Ah, my dear," Marie-Claire's father had said sadly,

"That is a sentimental female's point of view. But men think differently."

"Are you suggesting that the Prince and Princess should part?" Marie-Claire had asked, horrified.

But he had refused to say more. He merely warned her that unless matters improved, she might find herself looking for another job and this time it would not be in Le Petit Palais.

About twenty minutes later, the young secretary took a message to her employer. Catherine, still waiting for Dominic, was in her bedroom lying down.

"The Professor was at home fortunately, Madame. He thanks you and asked me to tell you that he is flying down to Nice tomorrow to an important patient. He asks if he may come across to the Island to see your Highness during the afternoon."

Catherine sat up. Her fingers nervously clasped the worn shabby little body of the White Monkey. Her eyes were suddenly big and bright. She said:

"Tomorrow! That's wonderful news, Marie-Claire."

But when Dominic joined her, she told him nothing about the letter, or the Professor's forthcoming visit.

For the first time in their married life, she decided to keep an important secret from her husband. And for the first time during the last year at least, her spirits began slowly to rise out of the utter darkness of despair.

17

Catherine had decided to ring her cousin Belinda in London. She got through to her on the private line from Le Petit Palais. Belinda deduced from what Catherine had to say, that she had had a scene with mother-in-law and that they were not now even on speaking terms. Also that Dominic had had a show-down with Henri Leveuve and sacked him. This followed the Ministerial Conference which had taken place a few days ago. The National Council was still solidly behind the Prince, which was some consolation, Catherine said, but he was in the unhappy position of being able to trust nobody now and especially not his Minister of State, although at the moment it would not be tactful to sack de Reynard after the Leveuve episode. The latter apparently had been caught red-handed by Dominic. Remembering Catherine's warning, Dominic had had his secretary closely watched. An astute and vigilant under-secretary informed the Prince that a carbon copy had been taken of the very secret discussions and decisions at the Council meeting, and conveyed to the Dowager Princesse. Before he could get as far as the Villa, Dominic had sent for him and accused him. Even Leveuve had been unable to lie his way out then.

When Dominic told his mother that Henri had been sent packing there was a ghastly quarrel. She tried to prevent it but Leveuve had to go.

"Poor Dominic," said Catherine, "is at his wits' end to know what to do with that mother of his, because he knows now how far she has gone beyond the bounds of propriety in her behaviour—all tied up, of course, with her power-complex and her hatred of me."

"Oh, darling, and what now?" Belinda asked.

"God knows," was the reply, "Dominic likes to lean on me and yet I am the one who stands in the way and seems to cause all the trouble."

"I'm sure you exaggerate. It can't be so."

"I'm losing my nerve," Catherine said with a brief laugh that held little of the joy which Belinda was so used to associating with the Cath. she knew.

Catherine added that she had recently sent for a certain Swiss Professor, full of hope because he had informed her that he might be of help. He had some new wonder-drug, connected with fertility. She had finally agreed to injections. But hope was fading fast.

"Everything seems to be going wrong, Belinda," she said.

Belinda spent the next few minutes arguing against this, and trying to bolster up her cousin's morale.

"It isn't like you to be a defeatist, Cath. Keep your chin up. I'm sure it will all be okay in the long run."

Now Catherine laughed with more spontaneity.

"I'm better already just for speaking to you. Nothing seems real any more out here except that I love my husband as much as ever and I'd give my whole soul to be a help to him instead of a sort of menace."

"You aren't—you couldn't be," Belinda protested.

But today in the magnificence of her Mediterranean palace Catherine still felt depressed and unsure of herself following that telephone call to her cousin.

There was no doubt, she thought dismally, that her childlessness had stirred up grim feelings and they were settling like a horrid veil over the radiance that had once been hers in Montracine.

She faced the fact that she was never really happy now unless she was alone with her husband and close to him. Only when she lay in his arms in the darkness and peace of the night, could they shut out the shadows. Then she felt almost happy, and secure again.

It couldn't go on, she thought; something would have to happen. Last night she had to face up to a banquet in honour of Isabella's birthday which had always been celebrated although it had taken second place to Dominic's once he became head of the Principality. But there had been a Bank Holiday for the people, and at night, in the palace, a Reception and dinner, attended by everybody of note in Montracine.

Isabella had not been able to plead illness or refuse to be present at this. Since Leveuve's dismissal a complete breach existed between herself, her son and her daughter-in-law, but she was still a patriot, and she believed, a personage to be reckoned with in Montracine. So she had put on a new gown and worn her famous diamonds and presided at the table beside her son; bestowing only the most glacial smiles on the young Princess at the other side of him and avoiding all speech with her.

Until the evening ended and Isabella was alone for a moment with Catherine then she directed the usual venom against her.

"You are looking ill and haggard, my dear. I would suggest a long holiday in your beloved London. Perhaps the climate of Montracine does not really suit you."

Catherine trying not to shrink from the bitter hatred in the elder woman's eyes, had squared her shoulders and answered:

"Perhaps not, Maman, but my home is here with my husband."

Isabella leaning closer, added in a low tone:

"If you really loved him as much as you say you do, you would not continue being such an embarrassment to him. Perhaps if you were no longer here —"

Catherine had broken in with passion:

"If I were not here he would be utterly miserable."

"But he will be more so if he is forced to follow others whom we know, into exile," said Isabella, with her icy smile.

Catherine had no time to protest that such a thought was outrageous, and that it was most unlikely that Dominic would ever be exiled. She wanted to tell Isabella that there might be a few rebels but the little Army, and Navy *and* the National Council were solidly behind their Prince.

As usual, Catherine did not wish to add to Dominic's troubles by repeating what his mother had said, but she lay awake for hours after Dominic slept, remembering it all . . . her nerves in shreds . . . her emotions confused. Could it be possible that Dominic *would* be better off without her? Divorce would not be looked upon kindly by their Church but would it be possible for their marriage to be annulled on the grounds that she had not given him an heir? Would he then marry again in order to have children? Would he learn to forget her in time – or at least stop mourning for her – and give himself entirely up to his people, as many another Crowned Head had done?

Dominic had woken up and found her sobbing. She would not tell him why. He drew her close and kissed her like the passionate lover who had once convinced her that he truly needed her. The adoring husband, on their honeymoon, in that heavenly chalet up in the mountain where they had known such happiness.

She clung to him and he kissed away her tears and whispered:

"Stay close to me, my Catherine. You are like a wonderful magical anchor in a bitter sea."

Later when she was calmer, he had murmured:

"Let me hear one of your verses. Repeat it to me in that beautiful voice of yours, please! It will soothe me."

So she had quoted one of her favourite and perhaps most poignant poems by Humbert Wolfe:

> "*Give me this promise! To be never*
> *the same. Or rather swear*
> *it shall not be this evening on this river,*
> *and I not there*
> *Look not, if you must look, thus stricken*
> *with midnight on your lips, nor close*
> *your eyes against the light when new lights quicken,*
> *And my light goes.*
> *Give me this promise, that hereafter,*
> *whatever may be lost along the years,*
> *no one but I will ever hear this laughter,*
> *nor staunch these tears.*"

The next day Catherine knew what she wanted to do. Ever since that poor little boy had been killed when the workers had marched into the port, she had longed to go down and see the parents, despite the fact that Dominic had begged her not to do so. She had been haunted by the thought of the mother's grief, and so deeply disturbed because the beautiful flowers she had sent for the funeral had been returned to her with a card that said: "*This cannot bring back our son.*"

Simply dressed, she drove herself down to the square and entered the Pâtisserie, where she found the child's mother, Madame Mévértes, alone. Madame greeted the girl pleasantly, but as soon as Catherine removed her sun-glasses, the woman gasped and her smile faded.

"I would rather not speak with Your Highness," she said none too pleasantly.

Gently Catherine assured her that there was no reason to look upon her as an enemy, and that she personally, was not responsible for what had happened.

Madame interrupted shrilly:

"Will Your Highness kindly leave my shop. It would make my husband angry to find you here."

Shocked and dismayed, Catherine begged her again to believe that neither she nor Dominic were responsible for the poor child's death.

Madame tossed her head.

"Maybe. But there are things going on around here that none of us like. Our Prince was all right until he married but—" she broke off and Catherine stood speechless, feeling sick and suddenly bitterly afraid for the man she had married and loved so much. Madame eyed the English girl with a gaze half sullen, half worried. Maybe it wasn't the Princess's fault that she had no child, but Gaston, Madame's husband, had it fixed in his mind that it was the Prince's marriage that had not only caused a clash between the National Council and the workers, but greatly reduced his popularity. Madame was a stupid rather spiteful woman and she decided to speak her mind.

"Oh, the Prince is all right," she repeated, "but if he dies, there are few of us want his cousin to take over. Besides, us people in Montracine were bent on a son being born to the royal family to inherit from His Serene Highness."

Catherine's heart seemed to plunge. She froze, while the woman added that she was sure her little Bruno would never have been lost if it hadn't been through all the trouble caused by His Highness's childless marriage.

Suddenly Catherine could bear no more. She turned and ran out of the shop, blinded by the scalding tears that poured down her cheeks. As she went, she heard the baker's wife screaming, uncontrolled, hurling another barb at her:

"Our Prince should have married one of his own kind instead of an English miss."

Catherine put both hands to her ears. She ran on through the brilliant sunshine as though pursued – stumbled into her car, and drove herself back to Le Petit Palais. She was trembling violently.

All the sweetness and warmth of that night she had spent in Dominic's arms, when she had whispered those lovely words of Wolfe's poem to him, seemed totally destroyed. The shopkeeper had told her the truth, she thought. The terrible truth that she had tried to ignore, although for a long time it had lain there deep in her mind. She had failed to give Montracine an heir and because of it, his people had turned not only on her, but on Dominic!

She cried wretchedly as she drove that car up the steep hill. Bit by bit, her anger, her indignation, turned to despair. Futile to tell herself that the baker's wife was a little crazy after her tragic loss of her boy. Or feel quite satisfied that had Dominic married *'one of his own kind'*, *she*, too, might not have borne him a child. The terrible fact remained that *she*, Catherine, had failed her husband and that she must not stay with him. *If* she went away, Dominic would suffer – yes, but he, too, would finally have to admit that she would ruin him and his beloved Island if she stayed.

Fate had been cruelly perverse, given them everything but the heir who was of such vital importance. Now it seemed she had brought catastrophe to the man she adored.

Again and again, Catherine thought also of those words that Isabella had recently said to her: "*If you really loved him as much as you say, you would not continue being such an embarrassment to him.*" And Isabella had added that he might be forced into exile, like other royal princes before him, if there was no heir.

Catherine was beaten. Broken on the wheel of her very

love for Dominic. So now she knew what she must do. She must go away, at once. And if necessary, if it was really for the good of Montracine and Dominic, she must stay away.

By nature, Catherine was a practical girl with an intelligent and modern mind but the events of this last year had done much to unnerve her and destroy her natural serenity. Her intense love for Dominic, their whirlwind courtship and her magnificent marriage, had once seemed to offer all the happiness in the world. Now like a glorious bubble it was bursting at her feet. She knew that it was not her fault that she had no child; but great harm psychologically had been done to her, first and foremost by Isabella and then by the uprising, following upon the heels of those fruitless agonising attempts to find a cure for her sterility.

She was in a state bordering on hysteria when she found a suitcase, and without ringing for a maid, or for Marie-Claire, packed it and changed into a suit for travelling. Then she, herself, telephoned to the Captain of the Prince's Flight.

"I have received bad news from London – personal news – I wish to be flown to England immediately," she said.

The answer was swift and courteous.

"*Mais oui, Madame la Princesse – tout de suite.*"

"I will drive down to the aerodrome now," she said.

In this crazy state she had only one clear idea, to leave Dominic and Montracine. To begin with, she must lie; make an excuse which would sound reasonable enough to prevent him from following her; for the present, anyhow. She would leave a letter telling him that a friend in London was dangerously ill and had asked to see her, and that she would keep in touch with Dominic and let him know her address and immediate plans.

She knew that this would distress him; that he would not like her going away. But he would not stand in her light. He would be sympathetic and kindly, as always. Above all things, he believed in the individual's right to be free.

Later when she was back in the old country she would think things out and decide how and when to make the permanent break. In a less tense hour, a more tolerant mood, Catherine might have stayed. But she was totally convinced that in this moment her decision was right and for the good of the man she adored.

She did not expect Dominic to be back in Le Petit Palais until later this evening. From La Cina he was going to a meeting of workers on the other side of the Island.

She finished packing before noticing that she had left the toy that old Augusta had given her on her pillow. The absurd white monkey, the mascot of Dominic's childhood. *Her* talisman.

Suddenly she picked it up and held it to her cheek and for a few moments wept bitterly. Through the tears, she stared around the beautiful bedroom which she and her husband had shared for so long; where there had been so much love —such complete fulfilment for both of them. It seemed to her ghastly that it should have all ended in this. She knew she could not face him, nor hear him beg her to stay, otherwise she would weaken. She must get away before he came back.

Hurriedly she packed the monkey. But there were no tears in her eyes as the beautiful aircraft which Dominic had ordered in England soon after they met, circled around the Island then, gaining height, moved out over the blue shining sea. She was beyond tears. She felt very tired and drained of emotion. Quite dispassionately she considered what she was doing; even wondered whether she had taken the coward's way out by deserting her post, or whether it was not, perhaps, the most courageous action of her life. She decided that it was the second of the two. For his sake she was leaving everything on earth that she loved most—Dominic and his Island—the fabulous Island which had become hers, but now, so heartlessly rejected her.

When they reached London Airport, the nice young Montracinean Captain who knew Her Serene Highness well and was one of her great admirers, asked when she wished him to return for her.

Her face was like a mask but she managed to give him a set little smile.

"I will let you know, Monsieur Roget," she said.

He saluted and left her.

Before she mixed with the crowd—once more the old Catherine she used to be, just nobody in particular—she stood watching the jet as it soared up into the clouds for the return flight.

Then the tears began to roll down her cheeks again and she felt a pain, a sense of desolation so acute that she almost rushed to the nearest telephone-box and put a call through to Dominic.

She could not believe that she had left him and would never ask Captain Roget to fly her back to Montracine.

18

"You can't go on like this, Catherine, you just can't!" said Belinda.

Catherine had been there nearly a week. Every night, Dominic telephoned his wife. That was the only time when Catherine came alive again, but she spoke in an artificially bright voice and kept struggling with the story of the mythical sick friend.

Yes, the friend was still at death's door, and she didn't want to leave London yet. Yes, she, herself, was fine, but missed him terribly. Yes, she must stay in London.

All this and more, amounting, as Belinda had told her cousin once or twice, to nothing. For she must know, in her heart, that if and when she told Dominic that she did not mean to return to Montracine, she would place him in a hideous position – worse than the one he was in now.

"You'll make him feel that he must definitely choose between you and Montracine. You'll play right into his mother's hands too. At the moment he hasn't a doubt in his mind about you. Why put one there? He'll only fight against it and suffer all the more."

This morning Belinda could hardly bear the sight of the distraught expression in Catherine's wonderful eyes. The girl was driving herself crazy. Like a squirrel in a cage, her thoughts turned round and round.

She seemed to Belinda to be oblivious even of her altered appearance. She was no longer her old immaculate shining self. She had always looked so radiantly beautiful and happy during these last three years, Belinda thought sadly. A princess in the most magical sense of the word – living blissfully in her enchanted palace.

But Catherine this morning was just a miserable, even untidy-looking girl – with hair that wanted setting, and no make-up on her face.

Belinda washed up a few pans and dishes, then shook her head at her cousin.

"For the umpteenth time, honey, you *can't* go on like this. For God's sake, when Dominic phones you tonight, tell him this fictitious friend of yours is out of danger and that you're flying home."

But Catherine rejected this suggestion. There were too many voices whispering in her ear. The voice of her mother-in-law accusing her of having ruined Dominic's life – warning her that she was about to bring the dynasty to an end if she stayed with him under the present circumstances.

"I can't. I can't go back and destroy him."

"You're round the bend, darling. You're destroying him now, *and* yourself."

"I don't believe that. He'll get over losing me and marry someone else."

"But you won't get a divorce."

"Something can be arranged. He won't be the only prince to take a second wife because he needs an heir."

"I give up," said Belinda with a sigh, "I'm off. It's my morning at the W.V.S."

After Belinda had gone, Catherine sat alone. It was such a ghastly muddle, she thought. But Dominic, the only man she would ever love, must come first. She *must* put herself in the background. She felt extraordinarily lonely. The week she had been away from him seemed like a century.

That night, when Dominic telephoned her, she went on

playing for time. When she returned from that call to join James and Belinda, there was a new hardness in her eyes. She told them that she was sure now that she was doing the right thing. Quite unconscious of the reason for her departure and of the state of her mind, Dominic had just told her that things seemed better in Montracine. He and his mother had also achieved some kind of reconciliation, which pleased him. They had dined together last night, and Maman had expressed the wish to end the breach with her daughter-in-law.

"This, of course, I don't believe. She's just cashing in on my absence," Catherine told the Holts. "But it appears that Dominic has had several meetings with the workers in the Italian zone and calmed them down."

They were to get higher wages and work fewer hours, following the world pattern of today. And during this last week when Dominic drove through the streets he had received a warmer welcome than he had been given for some long time.

"I know you will be pleased about it when you come back, my darling," he ended the call, "so come quickly."

"What did I tell you?" exclaimed Belinda.

But Catherine shook her head.

"On the contrary it proves to me that I ought to stay away. The Island is better without me, and Dominic will soon regain his old popularity."

Nothing would drive that belief from her mind. James and Belinda gave up trying. But when Catherine said that of course she must not encroach any longer on their hospitality and was going to an hotel, they both protested strongly. They had a spare room. It was hers for as long as she wanted it, and they liked her being with them. But once she said good-night and went to her room, they were both well aware that it was only to cry her eyes out. And they both agreed that there were dark and even desperate days ahead of Catherine unless the situation changed.

But it worsened. For a further week Catherine fought the demons of doubt and misery in her mind and continued to stall Dominic. Homesick she certainly was—miserably so. Each time Dominic spoke to her in that rich tender voice of his, begging her to fly back to him soon, she weakened. When he began to express concern and even doubt as to why this 'dying friend' should keep her away so long, she found it hard to pacify him. He was almost cross with her.

"Really, darling, this devotion on your part is very sweet and typical of you, but do I not get a look in? Le Petit Palais without you is like a morgue. And I cannot fly over to you at the moment because things are still too tricky here."

A few days later, Catherine caught a really bad cold and went to bed with a temperature. Belinda spoke to Dominic when he telephoned that evening. The doctor just wouldn't hear of Catherine flying until she was better, she told him, as the poor girl's sinuses were affected.

"My poor Catherine, kiss her for me and give her all my love," said Dominic.

Belinda put down the receiver and drew a long sigh.

"Poor Prince," she said to herself. "Poor Princess! Thank God, James and I are just two little nobodies and have our two lovely children as well."

But Catherine's sinus trouble became a genuine excuse for further delaying her absence from Montracine. The third week passed. Then there was a change of tone in Dominic's nightly calls to her. He sounded very worried. He presumed that the English papers had reported the fact that some ghastly kind of 'bug' had been hitting the Island for the last forty-eight hours. It was the children who were mainly affected. The schools were shut. All public institutions —libraries, cinemas, the theatre—were closing. A few adults were just beginning to succumb to the infection.

Hospitals were already crowded and the harassed doctors seemed unable to diagnose the infection or prescribe adequately. Even those they called in from the mainland had no definite ideas as to the real nature of the epidemic, which was as lethal as Asian 'flu. Physicians, nurses and the laboratories were working overtime.

Catherine, having now recovered from her chill, listened to this with a deep sense of alarm.

"Dear God – how ghastly, Dominic. And what about *you?*"

"I am all right," was his brief answer. "We all gargle and take precautions, but we cannot do much about inoculations or anything of that sort because they cannot diagnose the virus. Oh, it is frightful, Catherine! The poor little children – so heartbreaking. They just seem to drop down. They die in two days. Only the strongest recover."

"Oh, God!" repeated Catherine.

"On no account come back now," he added. "You are better in London, my Catherine. Incidentally, Maman is splendid. She has put on her old uniform of the Red Cross and works in the General Hospital every day. She is like the mother I used to admire as a child and whom my father always said was at her best in an hour of crisis."

When that call came to an end, Catherine went downstairs. The Holts were watching a television play. They switched it off as they saw her face.

"What's new?" asked Belinda.

She told them. They looked at each other, shocked. She continued:

"This is, of course, where I shall refuse to stay in England. Everything has changed. Whether I'm the right wife for Dominic or not, there is no doubt as to where I should be at this moment. Montracine is my country. If my people are stricken like this, then I must be there to do as my mother-in-law is doing – help with the nursing. I must be at Dominic's side."

Silence. Again James and Belinda exchanged glances. Then Belinda got up and put her arms around her cousin. She kissed her on both cheeks.

"You're a brave poppet. I always knew you were."

Catherine hugged her in return.

"Darling, I'll never forget how marvellous you and James have been to me."

James said:

"Wish I could help. From the doctor's point of view I shall be interested to know what this bug is. Let us hear, Cath."

After that, for Catherine it was one mad rush. But later she thought how amazing it was, really, that within such a short time she found herself in a Comet, flying to Nice.

She had told nobody on the Island that she was going over and she couldn't have borne to have waited for Captain Roget to fetch her. There was a spare seat, tourist class, on the big B.E.A. aircraft and she took it. Not a soul who looked at the slim beautiful girl, so quietly dressed, so reserved, could guess that this was Her Serene Highness, Princess Catrine of Montracine. On her lap as well as her purse was a B.E.A. bag which held only one thing, a little woolly monkey. Now and then, sadly smiling, she said:

"You've let us down, little one. You were supposed to bring us luck or, perhaps it *is* lucky that something has happened to take me back to *him* . . ."

Once in Nice, Catherine drove in a hired car to Cannes. From there she took one of the Hovercrafts that crossed to the Island. On this occasion she was recognised by the Captain.

"Your Serene Highness —" he began, red and stammering, but she put a finger to her lips.

"Please no. I don't want any publicity. Just tell me – how are things on the Island?"

"Bad, Madame, alas! Many deaths, mostly among the children. But now the adults too, are succumbing. It was said on radio and television last night that the Prince, in agreement with the Navy, is considering a quarantine. Except for necessary commercial traffic, all further tourist activities will be forbidden if things do not improve."

Catherine sat watching the water leap high in the air as the Hovercraft sped across the sea. Her heart was heavy – she was full of distress for the Island, but her eyes were bright. It was extraordinary, she reflected, only yesterday she had been sunk in the deepest gloom, feeling as though she had lost a limb – several limbs – by tearing herself away from her husband. English though she was, this afternoon she felt like a true Montracinean, returning home. Thank God she had made this decision!

The tears stung her eyelids once she first saw the familiar curving coastline of Dominic's Principality. How beautiful it looked in the brilliant sunshine. The mountains were deep purple. The little Port which they were rapidly approaching, looked so charming with the white, sun-washed walls – the old stone-quay – the little painted boats. But when she landed she felt a difference in the atmosphere. The whole place seemed empty, only a few officials and sailors were there to receive the Hovercraft.

With the help of the young Captain to whom she had spoken on board, Catherine passed quickly through the barrier, and found a car and driver. She was horrified to see the deserted streets. Desolation had fallen upon Montracine. There were only a few vehicles and bicyclists and one or two women, wearing black, with scarves over their heads, going in and out of the shops. Most of the cafés and stores were closed. The Square was empty.

Catherine thought: *This is terrible – unbelievable!*

The only sight that gave her any feeling of comfort, of cheer, was finding Dominic's own personal car in the court-yard outside Le Petit Palais. That, at least, meant that he was at home.

As she walked into the hall, she was received by two members of the palace staff who looked surprised to see her. They bowed low.

"*Bonjour, Madame la Princesse.*"

"Where is His Highness?" she asked.

"In his rooms, Madame. He has just finished lunch."

Catherine ran up the stairs to Dominic's suite. Her heart was beating like a sledgehammer. She felt she could hardly breathe. The next greeting she received was from the big wolfhound, Maxie, who lay stretched outside Dominic's writing room. The fine dog had become friendly with Catherine since her marriage and used to following both her and his master when they walked in the grounds. She bent to pat him, whispering: "Good boy, Maxie." Since the other hound, Sulla, had gone down to live at the villa with Isabella, Maxie had seemed lonely.

She opened the study door. She guessed where Dominic would be – more than likely, at this time, on his balcony under the awning, having coffee and a few moments' rest after his hectic morning's work. Or he might even be sleeping, used to the customary siesta. He had probably been up all night, struggling with the affairs of administration.

She found him, as she had half expected, sitting on the balcony. But he was not resting. He was writing, busily.

"Oh, Dominic!" she said, her whole heart in her voice.

He turned swiftly. She was shocked by the sight of his face – white, haggard, changed. His eyes widened with astonishment and delight as he saw her. He dropped his pen and sprang to his feet.

"*You!* My Catherine! Oh, *mon Dieu!* . . ."

Then she was in his arms. They were clinging together like two castaways on a desert island who had just discovered each other. His kisses rained on her upturned face. He kept repeating her name.

"Catherine! My Catherine . . .!"

She cried, there in his arms, with her wet cheek pressed against his. She cried with the sheer bliss of being back with him again, and with remorse because she knew now that she should never have left him – never have allowed his mother or the voice of the people or anything else in the world to have driven her away. Her place was here at his side.

Dominic was like a man delirious with happiness.

"It is such a shock – such a marvellous shock. I told you not to come."

"I'd have done anything else you asked but not that. I cannot keep away from you now that things are so bad. I must be here to work with you for the good of our people."

He calmed down, took her by the arm, and led her out on to the balcony.

"You must be so tired. Come and have coffee, my darling."

"I don't want anything. I had a meal on the Comet."

"Your poor friend is – dead?"

She crimsoned and turned her head away from him. She felt ashamed of all her lies, but she had meant it for the best. She did not want to tell him why she had gone to London and stayed there. This was not the time. She avoided answering his question and he had so much to tell her that he forgot he had asked it. He wanted to pour out the news about Montracine.

The terrible virus was rampaging through the Island and

the mortality among the children, especially the babies, was increasing. But the doctors were hopeful, he said. They had wonderful friends among all nations, offering nurses and medical men, placing their laboratories at the disposal of the experts here. Already two of the leading professors from the Montracine General Hospital had flown to Geneva. Many years ago Geneva had experienced an epidemic that was similar to this one and it was hoped that the professors would return with a new antidote to the virus.

"Where should I be of most help?"

Dominic took her hand and kissed it. Now that some of his joy at her return was diminishing, he looked desperately tired, she thought. Her poor darling! He began:

"You must not risk —"

"Don't tell me not to take risks, Dominic," she broke in. "I have come back with every intention of helping and I would not be worthy of my position as your wife if I sat safely in England."

Dominic sighed.

"I suppose you are right."

"Which area is the most seriously stricken?"

"The Italian zone. Maman is there every day and as I told you on the phone, she has been splendid. In a queer way it has been good for her, Catherine. She is softer, more gentle, more sympathetic. They are singing her praises wherever she works. She has even expressed a hope that you would return soon. She will be glad to find you here."

Catherine made no answer. She accepted what Dominic said with some reservation, knowing her Isabella, but she had every intention of doing the best she could on her part to keep the peace.

"There is one thing I have to tell you—one might almost call it a dreadful retribution," went on Dominic.

"There have been only a few deaths among adults. Those who have been sick have recovered fairly rapidly. But two men in the Italian zone died and one of them was Luigi Moldini, the ringleader."

Catherine gasped.

"Dominic! How awful! He was our enemy but one can hardly think of that strong craftsman as dead."

Dominic sighed.

"He – and others. We have been living in a nightmare, my darling. So much has happened on our once peaceful happy Island that seems unbelievable. Moldini's death was, I believe, partially due to his own excesses. He drank too much. The constant drinking weakened his constitution and affected his liver. They could not save him. I went to his funeral," he added sombrely.

"You *would*!" said Catherine. "The Moldini family must have appreciated the presence of their Prince who had little cause to lay a wreath on Luigi Moldini's grave."

Dominic sighed again.

"Let us try to forget it and all that went before it. He was a troublemaker and is best lying in peace where he is now. Since his death there has certainly been a better atmosphere in the factory at La Cina and no more hostile marches. Whether that is because of the plague or because the workers have appreciated that I am trying to meet their demands, I do not know."

"The plague!" Catherine repeated the old-fashioned word, shook her head with a faint smile, and laid her cheek against Dominic's shoulder. With every moment that passed she felt a deeper joy because she was with him. She would never leave him again.

She said:

"I must phone the Matron at the General and see if I can help with the babies there. I can at least wash and feed them and leave the trained staff more time for their medical work."

"Maman tells me that the great shortage is for Visiting Nurses in the homes where people are looking after their own invalids. But you must not enter infected houses —"

"I must and I shall," broke in Catherine calmly. "I can visit cottages and flats just as easily as any district nurse. There would always be something I could do."

Dominic sat watching his wife as she opened cupboards and drawers to look for fresh clothes – a cotton frock, an overall, a scarf to tie back her thick long hair.

"You are wonderful," he said. "You come back to work and take this thing without question."

"Darling, I must. Actually I shan't waste time phoning – I'll go straight to the General."

He beckoned to her. When she reached him, drew her into his arms and kissed her lips.

"Thank you for everything, my Catherine, and never leave me again for so long."

The tears stung her eyelids.

"Don't you remember our song – our record in the chalet – '*Je reviens te chercher*'? I will come back to find you!"

He nodded and went on holding her close, his face hidden against her hair.

She added:

"I always knew a love like ours could never die."

19

The thrill of Catherine's reunion with her husband had eventually to be replaced by the continued nightmare that had swept across the Island. For the next two weeks she worked from morning until nightfall. Although physically tired, her naturally calm, practical disposition helped her to face quite stoically the sight and sounds of suffering and the staggering change in her mode of life.

There were no more parties or receptions at Le Petit Palais. No more glittering public appearances by the Prince and Princess of Montracine.

While Catherine carried out the work appointed to her, Dominic was overburdened with the difficulties of many changes in his government and his own sharpened sense of responsibility. The general staff at Le Petit Palais was depleted by illness, and one of the major problems was in finding the right man to replace the First Minister, Gervaise de Reynard. 'The Fox', the man Catherine had never liked or trusted, terrified of the deadly infection, had made a cowardly exit from the stricken Island a week ago, taking his wife and three children with him.

This had flung the Council into confusion, and there were other deficiencies in the numbers of Ministers, due to the epidemic.

Never had Catherine admired her husband more. Dominic was magnificent. He did not spare himself. As for their private life, they saw little of each other except when the long anxious day ended, and they fell asleep, totally exhausted.

Catherine, with the help of the trained nurses, learnt how to cope with the sick, especially among the children who could no longer gain admittance to the already overcrowded hospital. She acted swiftly and organised a temporary hospital out of one of the big empty schools. At her side was the indefatigable Marie-Claire who exchanged her job as personal secretary for that of assistant to a hurriedly installed matron. Most of the trained staff came from abroad, including several Jamaicans.

It horrified Catherine to see how quickly the virus struck and how easily the more fragile of the children succumbed to it. No medicine, no antibiotics, proved of any use. The funerals were frequent and heart-breaking. Moving from one stricken home to another, Catherine made closer contact with the Montracineans than she had ever done. It was not long before they learned to accept her, not only as a makeshift nurse, but as a true friend.

If there had been any coolness or disinclination on their parts to receive her at first, things soon changed. The Madame Mévértes and her kind were in the minority. Soon the local paper which had not yet ceased publication, chronicled the fact that *La Princesse Catrine* had established herself firmly in the hearts of the people and they were deeply grateful to her. There was one photograph of her which Dominic cut out and treasured. Catrine, with a baby cradled in her arms, and the mother beside them – smiling because this little one, at least, had survived the horror.

The caption below said:

L'Ange de notre pauvre île – la Princesse Catrine. That was the name Catherine had earned: 'Angel of the Island'. Old wrongs, old sores, were forgotten.

Dominic was immensely proud of his wife but Catherine accepted no praise.

"I am only doing what anybody else would have done in my place," she said.

And when she was not working or sleeping, worn out, there was still time for her to feel that old anguished sense of guilt and despair because she had not given Dominic a son. What, she asked herself, was her present popularity with the people worth? She was still an inadequate wife for the Prince of Montracine.

Strangely enough, one of her greatest consolations during those tragic weeks on the sick Island was the new bond established between her mother-in-law and herself.

Montracine's agony had, as Dominic had told Catherine, made his mother a much more gentle and tolerant human being.

The first time the two women met again Isabella – looking, Catherine observed, very thin and sad – actually kissed Catherine on both cheeks.

"I am glad you have come, my child. Forgive me for the part I played in sending you away."

Catherine could only blush and stammer:

"Perhaps you were right – I suppose I *have* failed poor Dominic —"

"No," Isabella interrupted, "I was wrong. I should not have driven you away. Your absence has nearly killed him. And I know that you did not leave us because you had a sick friend. *I know* —"

"Please," said Catherine. "Don't ever let *him* know."

Then for the first time that Catherine could remember, her mother-in-law's haughty face was softened by a smile of genuine warmth. She took Catherine's hand and pressed it between her own.

"You are a good girl, Catrine. I have been very wicked.

And you were right about so many things. Even about Monsieur de Reynard. The coward! Running out of the Island like that with his family when my son needed him most. But I am the greatest culprit of all. I beg you to forgive me."

Stupefied, Catherine could only stare and stammer again.

Isabella was so changed from the old implacable enemy, Catherine could hardly credit it. This then was what trouble could do, it could bring people together, suddenly, marvellously. Out of misery there could come joy. For it was tremendous happiness for her to know that she could count now on Isabella's affection. When she suddenly dissolved into tears, it was the older woman who comforted her. Together, later on, the two of them left Le Petit Palais in Isabella's big car for the work which they were both doing without a single thought for themselves. Eileen Hallam, the wife of the First Secretary, showed her mettle as an Irishwoman by the unstinting help she gave to both Princesses, old and young.

At the end of another gruelling week a rumour spread around the Island that one of the professors in a Geneva laboratory had pinpointed the trouble and would be ready within another twenty-four hours with an effective remedy. It was, as they had thought, no ordinary virus but something more in the nature of Asian 'flu, only with a difference – a difference which they were now able to pin down and nullify.

After receiving this news, Dominic slept well for the first time since the catastrophe had overtaken his Island.

For so many bitter nights Catherine had watched him going downhill. Soon he was the old Dominic – bright-eyed – full of renewed vitality and enthusiasm. She clung to him; he held her close in his arms. She felt the wetness of his own tears against her cheeks.

"Oh, my darling!" she said, "my poor darling Dominic, how you must have suffered. But now there's so much hope, please, please, let me hear you laugh again."

He tried to laugh then, unashamedly blowing his nose.

"So you shall. We will laugh together often, darling."

"The Swiss are so clever with these things. I think we can safely believe that all will be well," she said.

He gave her a long deep look.

"*Mon Dieu!* And what a lot I owe to you, my Catherine. Without you I could never have got through those terrible days."

"What we must also thank God for is that you and the rest of us at Le Petit Palais have escaped," she reminded him.

"I agree, my darling, and when the whole thing is over, every church bell on the Island shall ring."

There were still anxious days ahead. Then the final victory. The Swiss preparations, flown to Montracine, proved no disappointment. The terrible epidemic was checked at last and after a further week of testing and treatment there were no fresh cases. The islanders slowly recovered. There had been many tragic deaths but at last it was over. The infant mortality had been high but seventy-five per cent of the older children who were stronger and more resilient, recovered. To each family where there had been death or illness, Dominic gave a generous sum of money from his own personal account in order to finance a free holiday for the stricken family.

Before the cooler days of November replaced the golden warmth of the autumn, life seemed almost normal for the Montracineans. Public places re-opened. Work was resumed. The fishermen put out to sea without wondering what fresh disaster they would find when they returned to harbour.

At the beginning of December, Dominic organised the first reception and dinner to be held in Le Petit Palais since the trouble began.

"We are going to celebrate," he told Catherine. "We are going to be *very* gay, my Catherine, and I shall strike one special, very secret medal in pure gold and pin it to the bosom of my beautiful brave wife."

Catherine smiled.

"I don't like *one* only. You must give one to Maman, too. She isn't as young as I am and you know she is terribly tired."

"You are a darling to think of her," he said and hugged her. "It shall be two medals, both the same."

But there was to be no further laughter or rejoicing after that happy hour Catherine and Dominic spent preparing a list of guests for the party.

With appalling suddenness, Catherine, herself, was taken ill. Quite well one hour, the next she had fainted and awoke to a temperature and violent sickness.

The news spread through Le Petit Palais like lightning. Faces which had been pleased and relieved before, grew long and grave again. Isabella rushed up from her villa with the palace doctor and an English physician who was on a visit to Montracine.

The focus was now entirely on Her Serene Highness Princess Catrine. Everybody was horrified – afraid that the ghastly bug had struck again, and right at the very heart of Le Petit Palais.

The Angel of the Island was dangerously ill.

For twenty-four hours Catherine, drugged by the physicians in order to relieve the blinding pain in her head, knew little of what was going on around her. Only now and again she became conscious of Dominic's strong fingers holding hers and his voice whispering:

"I am here, my Catherine. I am here. I shall not leave you. Do not leave me."

Then she would drift back into unconsciousness. At other times she opened her eyes to see her mother-in-law sitting beside her. Somehow the sight of that black garbed figure and the pale aquiline features which used to strike such dread in her, gave her a curious sense of security. The long thin fingers laid cool pads of *eau de Cologne* on her hot forehead, or now and then wiped the sweat from her face. Trying, in her own way, to be especially comforting, the Italian Princesse spoke in her daughter-in-law's own language.

"You are all right. I am with you, my child. Have no fear."

And Catherine, existing in a curious world of fantasy rather than fact, alternatively suffering and sleeping, dying and living, weeping and smiling, lay there just content to be taken care of. Catherine the strong and the brave, had become Catherine the helpless child. There was always a trained nurse in the background but it was these two—Dominic and his mother—she most needed, and they seemed to be there whenever she wanted them.

Once she asked for old Augusta. They did not tell her the sad news that poor frail Augusta had been one of the victims of the sickness that had spread across Montracine. They did not tell her anything that might upset her. And for Dominic it was a miracle that the marvellous Swiss preparation that had brought the epidemic to an end had come in time to save the life of the woman he loved so dearly.

Catherine recovered slowly but surely. She was young and strong and the strong will to live was there. Whatever her deficiencies, she knew now that she was totally necessary to her Prince and that if she died and left him he would be inconsolable.

The first time she was allowed to sit up and drink some of the excellent *bouillon* made for her by her head chef, Isabella sat near, embroidering and watching her daughter-in-law drink the soup. She had just placed a glorious fresh bunch of scarlet carnations beside her bed.

Catherine felt extraordinarily weak, and she was not yet hungry. She felt as though she had been very ill indeed, which was a new sensation for her. She had always been so well.

But for the first time today she asked her mother-in-law for news of her friends, and this Isabella took to be a good sign. Catherine was told that all was well with the people she knew and cared about. Eileen Hallam in particular had done a tremendous job. Her husband had just taken her back to England for a holiday, but they did not go, Isabella added, until they were quite sure Catherine was going to recover.

Marie-Claire, the little secretary, was a faithful, devoted friend and had been coping nobly with an immense correspondence. Letters had poured in from all over the world, wishing Her Serene Highness well. Le Petit Palais was full of flowers; many bouquets arrived daily by aeroplane.

"But," Isabella told Catherine, "I am only putting these carnations in here. Dominic brought them for you, himself, from Monte Carlo. The Rainiers gave him lunch yesterday. It was the first time he left the Island while you were so ill."

"My poor Dominic, is he all right?" asked Catherine anxiously.

"Perfectly. Thank God yours seems to be the last severe case and Dominic has withstood it altogether, like myself. We are what you English call 'tough'," said Isabella, smiling.

Catherine lay back on her pillows looking at her with wonder. Her mother-in-law was so utterly changed, so pleasant. Catherine broke out impulsively:

"Oh, Maman, I am glad we are friends now, you and I. I was very unhappy about my relationship with you."

Isabella came to the bedside, took one of Catherine's hands and looked down at it. It was a very thin hand. The girl had lost far too much weight, she thought. They would have to feed her up and see that she fulfilled no strenuous engagements for some weeks to come. She bent and touched Catherine's forehead with her lips.

"My dear – I have been a foolish old woman. Jealous and possessive and difficult. Things will be different now, I assure you."

After she had gone, Catherine lay still, waiting for Dominic. He spent as much time with her as he could – she knew that. Since her illness she had grown conscious of her own utter dependence upon him. It seemed to her now fantastic that she could ever have dreamed of leaving him

All was well. The winter sun was shining gently through the tall windows opening out on to the balcony. It was very peaceful here in her big beautiful room. Dominic's carnations were a glowing reminder of his love. She felt spoiled and content. Yet the tears were ready to roll down her cheeks and remind her that she was still weak. She thought:

Things will be different, Maman has just said so – yet they are really the same. The most important thing of all remains unchanged. My childlessness.

She heard voices outside the door, hastily dabbed her eyes with her handkerchief, seized a mirror and lipstick and made up her face, anxious that she should look her best for Dominic. She must not let him find her crying. It upset him so much when she was unhappy.

But it was not Dominic. It was an unexpected visitor – a tall fair-haired man whom she had never seen before. He was introduced by Isabella.

"This is Dr. James Vernon – one of your countrymen. I thought you would wish to see him. He has been staying with the Hallams. He is a cousin of Frederick's. He has been spending a holiday on the Island and would like very much to meet you before he goes home. He should have flown with the Hallams yesterday but stayed another day in order to meet you, *ma chère Catrine.*"

Catherine held a hand out to the young English doctor.

"I am delighted to meet you, Dr. Vernon. Thank you for coming."

"Forgive me if I leave you two," said Isabella. "I will have coffee sent to you. Yes, I see no reason why you should not have a coffee today, Catrine."

James Vernon sat down and smiled at the young English Princess. He had seen many photographs of her. The girl lying there in the big bed did not look well but she was even more beautiful than he had expected. What marvellous green eyes, he thought. What an enchanting smile.

They had plenty to talk about. The recent grave events on the Island; current affairs in England; the Hallams; and, of course, herself. But it was Catherine who brought up that subject rather than Dr. Vernon.

"You know of course about my personal tragedy?" she asked in a low voice.

"Yes, Madame —" he used the French title with the respect and homage due to her station.

"I refer, of course, to the fact that we have no child."

"Yes, Madame."

"Dr. Vernon, have you had many cases in your own life as a doctor – I mean – women patients who remain childless?"

He nodded, and looked away for a moment from those magnificent eyes which held such deep sadness.

"Yes, quite a few in my time, Madame. I am deeply interested in this work. I specialise in gynaecology and although my name is not at all well-known, I have a good practice in Penzance. I am a Cornishman," he added with a smile. "Freddie, my cousin, comes from Penzance, too, as you may know."

"I love Cornwall. I used to go there when I was a child."

The word *gynaecologist* always interested her. Dear God! How many of them had she seen and talked to! How many had held out hope, but no firm promises.

"It is unprofessional," she said, "but can you talk about *me*, Dr. Vernon? I mean, can you pretend for a moment that you are a visiting doctor?"

He had nice blue eyes and they looked at her now very gently, with kindness as well as homage.

"I should be honoured, Madame," he said.

"You don't know how hard it has been," she said, "but with my husband as ruler of this Principality—with the whole Island crying out for an heir—it's been pretty murderous for us both. He is so angelic, he never lets me feel responsible but I do."

"You are not responsible, Madame. You must *know* that when this unhappy state exists, it is due to no fault of either husband or wife. It is a matter of genes; nature chooses at times to be unco-operative."

"But with all the knowledge in the medical world today and with all these new treatments, why can't they help me?" Catherine asked wildly.

"Madame, tell me who you have consulted so far and what has been done. If it is not an impertinence on my part I would like so very much to know."

She never knew why, but she felt an extraordinary desire

to do as this young doctor asked, and to tell him everything. Strangers though they were to each other, there was some strange bond of sympathy between them. He was quiet, understanding; one of those rare people in whom one wishes at once to confide.

She answered his questions without reserve. Ill though she had been, weak though she still was, there seemed in this hour that a strange fresh vitality was flowing through her veins, strengthening her; making it possible for her to talk almost as vigorously as the Catherine she used to be.

She ended with the story of Professor Chambertin from Geneva who had come to see her three months ago and given her his new treatment. James Vernon listened intently. For a moment, after the Princesse stopped talking, he was silent. Then he said:

"Madame, may I ask you a few more questions? You have your own doctors, of course, I must not presume, but as I have already said, this is a subject dear to my heart. May I – ?"

"You may ask anything you wish," she broke in.

"I am not tiring you?"

"No." Then she added, with that smile he found so charming, "It's a subject very dear to *my* heart, too, Dr. Vernon."

He remained with her for nearly an hour and they talked earnestly. Finally the trained nurse who was still with Her Serene Highness, ventured to interrupt and suggest that Her Highness ought to rest.

When James Vernon left Le Petit Palais, driven in the Prince's car back to the Hallams' villa, it was to telephone through to the airport and alter his own plans. He was not going to leave Montracine this evening. He would stay another week, at the special request of Her Highness. A week which he had really meant to spend in Paris.

During his second interview with Catherine that following

morning, her personal physician was also present. Nobody else. There seemed a general air of mystery about the consultation. The nurse, and Catherine's personal maid, were given strict instructions not to mention it to His Serene Highness; and it was fortunate, perhaps, that Isabella did not come up from her villa, as usual. Another of her migraine attacks kept her at home.

Dominic was so tired when he came back to Le Petit Palais that he noticed nothing very different about the atmosphere surrounding his wife. He only knew that she was better – stronger – and, at last, eating solid food. This and the fact that life seemed to be returning to a state of health and tranquillity among the Montracineans. The two things of paramount importance to him.

He knew of course that Freddie Hallam's cousin, the English doctor, had called on her. His happiness, at the end of the week, knew no bounds when he first saw her on her feet again.

He had been away in Paris for the last twenty-four hours on urgent State business. He had returned late last night. It was one of those especially golden mornings of early winter which so often invested the Island with the magical glow of summer. There was no wind. The palm trees did not stir, and it was almost impossible to believe that in less than a fortnight it would be Christmas Day.

It was going to be a very special Christmas, Dominic had already told his wife and mother. In all the little churches where they had been praying continuously for the recovery of their Princess, there would be renewed prayers, at this time of thanksgiving, because she was well again. They would have a wonderful Christmas party in the palace with as many of their French and Italian friends and relatives, who cared to come.

But just how wonderful that Christmas was going to be,

Dominic did not realise until he came home to lunch on this memorable day.

He found his Catherine standing by the open balcony windows with the sun pouring in upon her. Dressing-gowns had been discarded. Today she wore slacks and a thick jersey with a polo collar. She looked to him like the young bride he had adored up there in the Alps on their honeymoon. And those wonderful green eyes of hers were shining so brightly when she looked at him that he felt his heart turn over. Oh thank God she was safe! he thought. If he had lost her how could he have endured it?

She came towards him, stopping first to put a half-smoked cigarette into an ashtray.

"Who told you you could smoke?" he began, reproachfully.

She put her arms around him.

"Don't scold me. It's my first."

"Do you really feel so well again?"

"Marvellous. I'm very strong, really, Dominic. I'll be right as rain by the end of this week."

He ran his fingers through her hair with all the old tenderness.

"I ask for nothing more but that you should keep quite well, my Catherine," he said.

"Are you sure that you could ask for nothing more?"

"But of course," he said, staring.

"Think again."

He frowned and laughed.

"*Je ne comprends pas,*" he said in French.

"You've got to tell me something that you want even more."

"But my darling, there could be nothing I want as much as your total recovery."

She dug both hands in her pockets, looking up at him in

a rebellious sort of way – like a schoolgirl rather than a serious woman who had been married for nearly four years.

She said:

"I know you're hungry and want your lunch and you must think I'm round the bend, but do try to think of something that you want just *as much* anyhow, as you want me to be fit again."

"You are speaking in riddles," he said. "Come on, now, what is this all about?"

"Isn't it your dearest wish that we should have a child?" she asked breathlessly. "A son, with any luck, to carry on the line?"

Dead silence. Dominic stood still as though she had transfixed him. His large dark eyes looked down at her flushed face with bewilderment. Then he said:

"Catherine – why ask me that? Why bring it up now? What possesses you?"

She drew a deep breath. The great secret that she had locked away in her mind and her heart for the last twenty-four hours must now break its bonds. It poured out. Clutching both his hands with hers, she hung on to them as though for support – as though her own excitement and rapturous happiness might take all the strength from her bones.

"Darling Dominic, it's happened at last! *I'm going to have a child.* It's happened at last, yes, *yes*, I tell you it has. There's no doubt about it. They have been taking tests. It's why Dr. Vernon stayed on. He's been in consultation with our own *médicin* and the professors. They are all quite agreed. I am three months pregnant. They say I'm a miracle because I ought to have had a miscarriage after all that work and worry, then my collapse. But you see how wonderfully women are made. They can go through ghastly catastrophes and still bring babies into the world. And I'm going to bring ours into our world, Dominic. Sometime in June. Such a lovely month, darling. Aren't we lucky? Our child will be born in the loveliest month at Montracine."

The words jerked out. She was half laughing, half crying, holding his hands, moving them to and fro as she spoke.

He never said a word. He was like a man stunned.

She took him by the arm, drew him to the chaise-longue by the window, and made him sit down. She sat beside him.

It was quite true, she went on more calmly, and the whole thing was due to that Professor Chambertin who had come from Geneva to see her over two months ago. She must then have been in the first month of pregnancy but the new fertility drug he had given her had ensured it. So they were twice indebted to Switzerland – for *this*, and for the victory over that terrible virus that had almost destroyed the Island.

But the funny thing was, Catherine continued, she had not dreamed that the miracle had happened. She had experienced no special signs of pregnancy such as morning sickness; true, she hadn't been feeling exactly well, but she didn't say so to anybody, because it hadn't seemed important. Then she had had that chill in London and afterwards all the work on the Island, so when she felt a bit dizzy or nauseated, she had ignored the symptoms.

And how had James Vernon come into all this? Well, he was a gynaecologist and although he had not the slightest intention of speaking to her professionally, she had encouraged him to do so. And it was her answers to his questions that had made him believe she ought at once to have a pregnancy test. He believed that nature and Professor Chambertin combined had worked the miracle. He was proved right. Of course even if Dr. Vernon had never come, she would have found out her condition sooner or later. But it was wonderful that he had proved it and brought her such happiness now when she most needed it. Brought this tremendous hope to them both.

"And it is tremendous, isn't it, my darling?" she asked Dominic. "We have everything in the world now, haven't we?"

Dominic was visibly pale and shaken. But his eyes were as bright as hers as he put his arms around her. He kept saying:

"*Mon Dieu!* Oh, *mon Dieu!*"

"We won't tell the people for another month," she said, holding his hand against her cheek. "We'll just make *absolutely* sure first, although they assured me this morning that there is no doubt, and quite frankly *I* know it's true. I'm quite convinced. But we'll only tell Maman now because she'll be so thrilled."

He let out a deep sighing breath.

"I cannot believe it yet, my Catherine."

"No, it's been a long time, and quite frankly I've often thought it would never happen. Oh, Dominic, if it's a boy, the Island will go mad. What shall we call him?"

"Dominic the Fifth, of course," said the prospective father loudly.

"And all those other names. All you Princes have so many names," she laughed.

"Edward shall be one, after your father."

"That's sweet of you, but supposing it's a girl?"

"I shall not complain. There is no reason why a Princess should not be the head of our Principality just as Elizabeth is the Queen of your great country."

"I will not consider having a daughter. It must be a son," Catherine said. "And oh, Dominic" – she spoke on a sadder note – "it grieves me that dear old Augusta will not be here to see him. But Little Monkey—well we must keep him wrapped in mothballs, mustn't we, for the second generation —" she was laughing again.

Deeply moved, Dominic sat for some long time, holding her hands, kissing them without speaking. Then he said:

"You will not smoke one more cigarette, my Catherine. You will drink only a little wine and you will take no exercise —"

She interrupted, putting a hand over his mouth.

"For heaven's *sake*, what sort of tyrant am I married to? *I* am not Queen Victoria and this is 1969. Exercise is very good for prospective mothers and there'll be no lying around for the mother of the future Dominic V. Is that clear, my darling?"

He shook his head at her.

"Very clear. My wife is a rebel. This is treason."

The beautiful green eyes sparkled at him.

"Come and have lunch. You must be hungry and I'm getting back my appetite—just a little wine and just one cigarette . . . yes?"

"Anything you want, my Catherine. I am so happy. I am so magnificently happy—I would like to give you the whole world."

"It is rather terrific," she whispered.

He drew a deep breath and nodded, smiling at her.

"That is the word. Ter-rific!"

Arm in arm, they walked through to the room where their meal awaited them.

. . .

In her Swedish kitchen in the little house in Holland Park, one fine morning in the June of the following year, Belinda sat at the table carefully cutting a paragraph out of her morning paper. Quite a considerable paragraph including two photographs, one of a very handsome young man in uniform; one of a lovely girl wearing court dress and a magnificent tiara.

Belinda with a smile on her face, studied the two faces, then for the second time that day read the caption aloud. Somehow it sounded more thrilling to repeat the words aloud than to read them to herself. In all conscience, she thought, it is thrilling enough.

"It is announced from the Island of Montracine that at 11 p.m. last night, Her Serene Highness, Princess Catrine, gave birth to a son, weighing eight and a half pounds. Both mother and son are doing well and the Island has been en fête *since the news was broadcast from the palace. The arrival of a son and heir has a special significance for the young Prince and his English wife because it is their first child after four years of marriage. The Queen and Prince Philip have sent a message of congratulation."*

THE END

DENISE ROBINS

JEZEBEL

Jezebel's reception into Samaria was hailed as one of the wonders of the world. Drenched in the exotic colours of the East, the spectacle of Ahab's bride and her triumphant progress to the Ivory Palace was never to be forgotten. Yet even then, amid the cheering voices, there were those who seemed to sense a dreadful power in Jezebel's stately bearing. Her beauty brought her praise and admiration from all who served her. But as Thamar, her half-sister had foreseen, the seeds of Jezebel's glory were later to bear a terrible fruit. For her evil and tyranny would one day earn her the title of the wickedest woman in the world.

'A brilliantly plausible re-creation – a fascinating achievement.' *She*

CORONET BOOKS

MORE ROMANTIC FICTION FROM CORONET